CHANGING LIVES
TALENT AGENCY SERIES
BOOK ONE

NICOLE EGLINGER

CHANGING LIVES

TALENT AGENCY SERIES

BOOK ONE

NICOLE EGLINGER

AUTHOR OF POPSTAR LOVER SERIES

DEDICATED TO THE LOVES OF MY LIFE
MYHUSBAND LES AND SONS CHAD, SHANE,
BRANDON AND JEREMY!!!

PROLOGUE:

My name is Makayla Rose Weiss; I am at the height of my career in Los Angeles as an entertainment manager and owner of the company. I mange many Movie Stars and Musicians. I have two older sisters who live in San Francisco Ashley and Jackie.

Both of my sisters were married and had kids Jackie had 3 kids their names were Jenna 14, Ben 10 and Megan 6. My oldest sister Ashley also had 3 and one more on the way their names were Gina 16, Thomas 15 and Kevin 10. I was always the free spirited one out of the bunch and enjoyed the freedom and putting my mark on this world. I enjoyed my career and my single life hanging with friends and living the high life partying and sleeping with whomever one or two men if I chose.

Never having to answer to anyone or for anything for that matter and was free to do whatever I choose, like traveling the world seeing new places and meeting new people. I remember my older sister Ashley would always rag on me because I haven't settled down and have a family of my own. I never wanted that it just wasn't me I only was responsible for myself. My older sister

Jackie understood where I was coming from and respected my decisions. She only wanted me to experience love and the miracle of life. She said it would help mold me into a better person whatever that meant.   Until I met a gorgeous dark hair, blue eyed Australian singer.

That was the day my life would change in more ways than one. I suddenly became in a sense obsessed and the day when I lost my heart. Then tragedy struck and that was the day I would come to remember all of my days. I knew

Jackie would have loved to see that day I would fell head over heels in love and would love to have met him.

Jackie and I were so close in most ways she was my soul mate especially when both our parents passed. That was until the unthinkable happened changing mine and the rest of my families lives forever.

CHAPTER ONE

I pulled up into my spot at my management agency in my red AMG Mercedes. I read my sign that adored my spot RESERVED FOR Makayla Weiss.

"God how I loved being me!" looking in my rear view mirror putting on my lipstick.

I checked my look in my rear view mirror how I loved my eyes as green as jade as the ocean and long blonde curly hair that was looking back at me.

"Hay Miss Weiss looking hot today!" Brent the security guard said while whistling at me.

"I know and you better get back to work stud… and by the way hay is for horses' thank you!" I replied as I entered the building flashing a smile over my shoulder.

No sooner did I make it to the reception area that was just outside my office Cyndi was motioning for me.

"Oh my god what is it now…I mean can't I get into my office first without you flagging me down!" I hissed rolling my eyes.

Just then I heard what sounded like a man clearing his throat as he Started walking towards me. I turned around to face this man as Cyndi was speaking to me.

"I'm Damian Starr…I believe we spoke on the phone!" He replied as he extended his hand out to me and flashes a 100 watt smile in my direction.

"Oh right…I remember your sexy accent…Australian right…umm… I must say some of my best lovers have been Australian!" I said in a pure flirty manner while sizing him up.

He chuckled at me and that is when I noticed how amazing he smelled of Dolce & Gabbana and that fresh showered and that manly scent that drove me crazy.

"Umm…follow me…Mr. Starr!" I murmured and meander through the door of my office. I tried to turn on the light but my hands were full of my briefcase, laptop and a purse and of course a coffee.

"Want me to help you Miss…hmm!"

"Yes…thank you… and please calls me Makayla!" I answered while placing my items on my desk.

I sauntered over to Damian and extended my hand out to him with a smile and he graciously took my hand.

For a moment I couldn't speak when he took my hand electricity course through my veins causing my thighs to become inflamed and a deep ache soar through my groin. I tried to ignore this wave of pleasure but then my nipples harden such *traitors I said to myself in my head* and cleared my head with a shake and a smile.

"So…umm … you are here because you need a manager as your normal manager…is now married and had a baby…and wants to have more time for them!" I spoke from my memory and flashed a flirtatious smile.

"Yes…I am…so tell me are planning an upcoming marriage or having a family any time soon!" he inquired as he grabbed my hand again and smiled.

I stood there looking him up and down going over his chiseled features and words with that sexy thick Australian accent in my mind's eye and his cock I meant cockiness and that amazing smiled.

"Me...be married or have a family...umm not my cup of tea mate if you know what I mean!" I alleged with a smile noticing his real engaging blue eyes.

"Great...I love Layne to death but I really don't want her to sacrifice her family for me...maybe one day I will have all the happiness she has...but I guess I haven't found the one yet!" he informed me with a smile still holding my hand.

"Well then if you want...I can help you out in that department...and whatever else you need!" I articulated to him and pulled my hand away and took a seat at my desk crossing my long legs in a sexy manner.

"Anything else I can do for you Damian...oh and by the way I'm one of your biggest fans!" I smiled at him not dropping my eyes off him.

"Umm...there is just one more thing...would you have dinner with me tonight!" he asked.

"I mean to go over...everything I expect from you!" he said with a cheeky smile.

"Umm...sure where should I meet you in your hotel room?" I whispered while pulling files from

my briefcase.

"Umm...I really don't know...I'm not from around here!" he said with a wink.

"I know how about...I pick you up here!" he said, as he was looking me over.

I didn't hear him, as I was busy pulling my laptop out of its case and plugging in the wires.

"Dam it …I need another plug!" I hissed while looking around under my desk for an extra outlet.

"Umm…Makayla there is one over here!" he said as he started looking around my desk.

"Thanks…new office…or should I say bigger office with a view!" I chuckled whilst crawling around my desk on all fours discreetly as I could in my skirt suit.

Damian was giggling under his breath at me as he was looking on. I finally found the plug but just one problem it was right smack dab in front of Damian. I got to my feet looking at him as he looked back at me.

"Umm…Damian please pardons my backside!" I exclaimed as I bent over in front of him.

"Mmm…not a problem from where I sit!" he said as he watched my ass.

I got a funny feeling like he was fighting with himself not to reach out and touch my ass.

"Oh my god!" was all I heard as he decided to get up and walk over to look out at the city below.

I knew he was liking what he saw and not to mention I was enjoying the sight of him and the scent of him too.

"Finally…umm…so where were we?" I asked as I turned around to face him whilst I decided to sit on the edge of my desk.

Damian came back over and sat down right in front of me. I couldn't help but noticed his starring on my legs as he took up occupancy in the chair.

At that moment all I could think of was what he would look like on his hands and knees looking up at me wondering if that sexy mouth of his would feel on my pussy lips.

"Umm!" he said as he cleared his throat as I reached for a sip of my coffee as a dribble fell on the corner of my red lips.

Without thinking I wiped the dribble with my finger and then sucked on it paying no attention to Damian.

"Oh my god…we were just sucking your lips…I mean talking about dinner tonight!" he exclaimed as his voice cracked.

"I will be here around sevenish…is that okay…I really need to go now!" He said nervously as he walked towards the door.

"I'll be here stud…I mean Damian!" I said with a hint of a flirty smile.

I watched his ass as he walked back towards the door as I quickly grabbed the file that was sitting on my desk to fan myself. I stood up quickly and just had to make a motion like I was grinding against his leg.

"Oh my god!" exclaiming under my breath at how gorgeous he was not realizing he had looked back at me over his shoulder to say something else.

He almost did a happy dance when he noticed my reactions were mimicking his same reactions he felt when he first met me face to face.

"Makayla, thank you for seeing me without an appointment…I look forward to having my way with you…I mean working with you!" he uttered and blew me a kiss and winked at me over his shoulder opening the door.

"Of course anytime Damian and will see you later on!" I stammered as my jade eyes captured his feeling my face flush.

I watched as he stepped through my office door and then closing it behind him. Strolling over to the door I leaned my head against the door and blew out the breath I didn't realize I was holding.

On the other side of the door Damian grabbed himself trying to replace his cock to a more comfortable place in his jeans and making sure his erection wasn't noticeable as he could feel himself throbbing.

His skin was on fire and he could feel his heart beating in his ears as he walked along the hallway and out of the building's front doors.

After regaining the strength back in my legs I walked over to the window and watched him get into a black limousine. I thought to myself how crazy I was acting I didn't want anything more than a fuck session from him.

I no more wanted to settle down or tie myself to any man as I wanted to go get a root canal. After I saw him get into the car I strolled over to my desk so I could start my day. Many times I found myself thinking about undressing Damian and I had to pull my attention back to my work.

"Miss Weiss… you have a meeting and everyone is waiting for you in the conference room!" Cyndi stated through the phone.

"Okay…thank you Cyndi!" answered her back and hung up the phone.

I gathered my files I needed for the company meeting to catch me up with the management personnel about the new scripts and go over new contracts that came in from all the movie studios and other sources.

I hated these meetings but I couldn't let any of my clients to get less than anything they deserved. I guess that is what happens when you are sought out and had waiting list that went on for miles. Not a day goes by that we aren't double booked and had clients begging us for our representation.

Also we needed to discuss a couple of charities events that we hold every year. All during the meeting all I could do is tap my pen against my palm mindlessly and get lost in a daydream of undressing Damian and having my wicked way with him.

God those amazing fuck me eyes looking up at me from his knees and running my fingers through his unruly blonde hair. Oh and that mouth such kissable and plump lips what I imagined his lips would feel like against my skin kissing me all over. Not to mention that thick Australian accent just talk to me baby and I'm dissolving into a puddle under my chair and orgasm city.

My thoughts were derailed before we got to removing clothing and I was brought back to the here and now by a colleague repeating her question.

"Makayla…is the Beverly Hills Country Club okay for the Children's Home Society charity event!" she stared at me with questions.

"Of course I think that would be fantastic…Kelly…and thanks for taking care of this event…you are a whiz…and it will be amazing!" I declared while I turned to the next thing on the agenda.

Kelly continued going over the details to the whole conference room. I listened but just barely my mind was filled up with other thought of a more intimate and lustful thoughts of later on tonight.

Two hours later and a variety of topics and about 20 some contracts later I get to go to another meeting across town. I rushed into my office to freshen up and grab some files off of my desk putting them into my briefcase. Walking over to my closet I pulled off my flats and put on my red stilettos and then I pulled on my skirt suite jacket.

 Grabbing my briefcase, I walked out of my office and over to my assistant desk and asked her to forward all my calls over to my cell phone.

"I will be back after my meeting!" I was cut off by the ringing of the phone.

"Miss Weiss office…how may I help you" I listen growing more annoyed by the minute.

"Yes…she is right Mr. Star …hold on one moment!"

I looked at Cyndi and was trying telling her silently I have to go and that I don't have time to talk but she ignored me. But I took the phone as I didn't want to jeopardize Mr. Starr's opinion about my firm.

"Hello…Mr. Starr what can I do for you?" I asked as a smile broached my lips.

"Well…I just wanted to tell you …how grateful I was to get some of your time this morning…and how I haven't stopped thinking about you all day…and that I'm so excited with getting to work with you company…but mostly I look forward to working personally with you!"

"Well thank you Mr. Starr…I do too but not to cut you off…but I have a meeting across town in like 50 minutes…see you later on Mr. Starr!" I said looking at my wrist watch.

"I understand and I will see you at your office Makayla…have a good meeting…see you later!" he said with a hint of a question.

I handed the phone back to Cyndi with the corners of my mouth turned upwards in a smile. I sashayed down the hall and got onto the elevator along the way I said hello to my various colleagues and employees.

Getting off the elevator I walked past the front desk and security staff as Brent came out from behind the desk to hold open the front door. Mostly I think it was so he could have a good look at my ass. I tell you all it took is just giving that man just a taste of me and he follows me around like a little puppy.

I smiled back at Brent and thanked him and walked over to my Benz and hit the button to unlock my car and got in. Made it across town in about 20 minutes which was very unusual in LA but I guess I was just lucky.

CHAPTER TWO

I was finishing up the contract when Cyndi came in.

"See you in the morning Miss Weiss!" she said as she placed some files on my desk.

"Umm…these need your signature!" she said as she looked at me.

"Okay…just leave them here …thanks have a good night…see you bright and early!" I said still looking down at my desk.

With that Cyndi left the office and I went back to my work. Just then my phone started ringing!

"Hello…Makayla Weiss speaking…how may I help you?" I said into the phone.

"Hello there sexy!" I heard Russell reply.

"Wow Russell…it has been a long time!"

"Yeah I know…so I hear you are hanging with Pop Stars now!"

"Yeah I am!" I chuckled as I started playing with a curl and put my feet upon my desk.

"Dam that is too bad…I really miss you!" he said.

"So do I!" I replied.

"Umm…I was wondering…do you think we could see each other soon…I really need you!" he said in a sexy voice.

"Or maybe you might want to accompany me to the Oscars and some parties…and you know what else!" he giggled.

"Ha…ha…you are too much Russell…I'll see Hun!" I said as I heard a knock at my door.

I turned toward the door to see Damian standing there. I motioned for him to enter my office and finished up my conversation.

"Umm…I will get back to you Russell by tomorrow!"

"Please…I really need you!" he replied.

"Me too…look I really got to go have a prior engagement…bye talk to you soon!"

"Looking forward to it…bye sexy!" he said and hung up.

"Sorry to interrupt…but your receptionist is gone!" he said with a smile.

"No problem…no sweat!" I said as I pulled my jacket off to reveal a slinky black dress as I pulled my hair down from the clip.

Damian was watching every move I was making intently.

 I pulled out my compact to fix my lips sensually as Damian ran his fingers through his dark hair.

"Omg…I mean where are you taking me?" he asked trying to change the subject.

"Oh right…I think Bree's would be nice …it's in Beverly Hills!" I said as I looked over at him.

"Sounds nice…I took the liberty of getting us a car!" he informed me.

"Okay…that is fine…ready when you are!" I said as I grabbed a shawl from my closet.

"Shall we!" he said as he entwined my arm in his.

I smiled as we entered the hallway to wait for the elevator still arm and arm as he rubbed his hand on top of mine. For some reason I felt so special the way we moved about the hallways.

But for some reason I was feeling butterflies in my stomach the way he touched my hand, in some ways this was quite different to me.

As we walked outside I noticed the driver opening up a door to a limo.

"Miss Weiss…Mr. Starr!"

"Thanks Ralph…Bree's Restaurant in Beverly Hills!" Damian said to the driver with a smile.

"Certainly…excellent choice Mr. Starr…know it very well!" he said as he closed the door.

~*~

CHAPTER THREE

In the limo I sat across from Damian watching his lips as he spoke to me. I looked around the limo taking in everything around us. From the plush leather white seats to the ambience of the rope lights that seem to light Damian gorgeous features of his soft plump red lips to his amazing blue eyes that seem to dance up my legs to my beautiful rosy red lips to my breast that were the perfect size and very perky. Just then I saw a lighting streak across the sky.

"Wow...looks like rain...and the traffic hasn't budged!" I said with a disappointed look.

"Yeah...I guess...umm relax we will get there in due time...I mean you have nothing else to do...besides we can find something to do!" he chuckled.

"Umm...I guess so!" was all I said as I continued looking about the car.

Soon my eyes caught a glimpse of a little bar. I moved closer to the bar as I watched Damian's legs stretch out extending almost to where I was sitting. I happened to spot a bottle of tequila with a tray of salt and some limes.

"I got something we can do!" I said with a smile as I raise my eyebrows.

"Umm...okay!" he said with a confused look on his face.

"I say we do body shots!" I grinned while looking at him.

"Umm...excuse me...body shots!" he said blankly.

"Do you not know what body shots are?" I inquired.

"Ha…ha…sure I know what they are!" he said with a chuckled.

"These windows are privacy glass right!" I asked as I tapped the window.

"Yes…but umm…what does that have to do with anything!" he said nervously.

I looked over at him with a smile as I moved closer. I stood up and hiked my dress up to above my thighs and seductively crawled up his legs.

Allowing myself to feel his leg against me. I notice him taking it all in nervously. Where I straddled him coming to rest right near his cock.

"Umm…Makayla what are you doing…correct me if I'm wrong we are on business!" he said with a hard swallow.

"Relax…what is business without a little fun…huh!" I said as I looked at him.

"Okay…I mean…umm!" he stumbled over his words.

I grabbed a piece of lime and offered it to him, which he disregarded it.

~*~

CHAPTER FOUR

"Bite this!" I demanded.

"What I'm not going to bite it…are you mad?" he said breathlessly.

"JUST BITE IT DAM IT!" I said forcefully.

"ALRIGHT…GEES…just no lady ever asked me to bite it before…and besides mum says it's not nice!" he said nervously.

I gave him the look of death and he finally took it and even offer up his neck. I almost took it but I had other ideas so I ran my tongue along his neck. At that moment I noticed another member had joined us in this game.

"Umm…what is that?" I asked with a grin I knew exactly what it was.

He looked at me with his engaging eyes soon my eyes met his. I Started unbuttoning his shirt all the way to the end leaving a trail of kisses along his torso. I could feel him tensing up and I soon assured him. I was almost to his pants when I felt him hold the back of my neck not sure what he wanted or if he wanted me to continue on, his anticipation was building. So I licked him just under his belly button and placed the salt whilst grabbing for the shot. I could hear him moaning under his breath. Then I came up and swigged the drink after licking the salt from him to meet the lime he was biting. To my surprised he dropped the lime and soon he engulfed my lips whilst letting his tongue meet mine. I leaned into him and accepted him.

It became quite intense I pulled back from his lips and touched mine.

I was so hot the need to have him was eminent almost a need no longer a desire. I pulled him to me again and kissed him passionately. Next thing I knew the car stopped and Damian pulled back grabbing at his shirt I had unbuttoned and Started buttoning it again. I stood up and moved off him and began fixing my dress.

"We are here!" we both said with a laugh.

"I swear it is like I'm a young man expecting to get caught with my pants down!" he chuckled.

The door opened and Damian got out first and reached for my hand to help me out. The driver closed the door as I moved out of the way.

Damian looked towards the building and was in shock.

"This is a hotel!" he said with a surprise as he looked back at me.

I put my back against the car door and smiled back at Damian.

"Yes…it is…but the restaurant is in the lobby!" I replied.

"Well should we eat or get a room?" he asked with a cheeky smile as he was still reeling from what happened in the limo.

Just then his lips engulfed mine again as I once again leaned in and accepted his. We stood there kissing and roaming each other's body.

Just then the sky opened up and poured but we still were deep in a passionate kiss. Shortly after Damian backed away to look at me.

"So should we eat or get a room!" he replied.

"Umm…what do you think?" I asked whilst putting his hand between my legs rubbing his hand along my clitoris.

"Umm…well I'm not that hungry anyway!" he smiled as he grabbed my hand and led me inside the hotel.

~*~

CHAPTER FIVE

I let him lead the way inside and over to the desk.

"Umm…we need a room!" he said with a crack in his voice.

"Certainly sir!" the man said with a smirk.

"We just arrived here…we are honeymooner!" Damian whispered as he kissed my lips again.

"Umm…okay sir…no problem!" he smiled as he took Damian's credit card.

The energy between us was so exhilarating I really didn't care if the whole world knew what we were about to do. All I knew is I needed him so badly my insides were screaming in anticipation. Next thing we knew is we were on our way to a room. We finally got to the room where Damian slipped the card key into the slot on the door. No matter how Damian tried he couldn't get the door opened.

"Shit!" he screamed.

"Give it here…I'll do it!" I laughed as Damian went on grabbing at my ass and rubbing himself against me.

"Omg…you are so hot…you are perfection!" he whispered.

I remember thinking to myself that I knew was hot and sexy. Finally, we got in the door when Damian pounced on my lips and me as he pulled my shawl off. After I helped him I engulfed his lips as with my foot I slammed the door shut.

"Oh god I need you so badly!" he whispered.

I pushed him back against the wall knocking off pictures as I dropped to my knees. I started undoing his belt and then his pants.

"Omg!" he moaned as he grabbed the back of my neck pushing me onto him.

With that I placed my lips upon his hardness and started licking and sucking while looking up at him.

"Oh god yes!" he moaned.

"Oh yes!" he screamed.

After a few minute he was putty in my hands.

I could feel the tension that was forming deep within. After a few Damian just seem to explode as he grabbed me tighter until the twitching subsides.

"You are awesome!" he said as he pulled me up to his lips.

"Thanks…but I'm not done with you yet!" I said with a smirk.

"Good cause I'm not done with you either!" he chuckled as he leads me to the bedroom and on to the bed.

He started kissing me as he unzipped my dress as it fell to the ground exposing my thigh highs and my black lacy bra and thong.

"Wow you are even more beautiful than before!" he whispered as he pushed me back on the bed after stripping the remainder of his clothes off.

I lay upon the bed waiting and thinking of things to come. Just then I felt his hands roaming my body followed by baby kisses along my torso. It seems to tickle with every kiss he burned into my skin until he abruptly pulled my thighs apart as he slipped my thongs off me.

"Mmm!" I whispered.

He stood there admiring me as if I was a satisfying meal.

"I'm so hungry!" he whispered.

"What now!" I screamed as I went on.

He placed his fingers to my lips and started kissing my torso again. This time he stopped when he got to my pussy and he began licking and sucking on my lips whilst rubbing my clitoris with his other hand.

He even decided to bite my lips a wee bit. All I knew is I was headed for orbit as the waves of pleasure besieged my body.

"Yes…mm…yes!" I whispered.

Not soon after he had brought me great pleasure. I rolled over onto his chest as I started kissing him again.

"So did I please you Makayla!" he asked as he took my hand.

"Yes…you are amazing!" I whispered as I looked over at him.

He pulled me into a hug whilst I straddled him.

"Makayla…you are so amazing!" he said as he ran his hand up and down my back tenderly.

I smiled back at him as I rubbed myself on his cock.

"Well…I see you want some more!" he said with a cheeky smile as he pulled himself up to me as our lips met.

He pushed me back onto my back where he started kissing and sucking my nipples and down my stomach. I decided to smack his ass as I couldn't resist it.

"Ouch what was that for?" he said as he rubbed his ass.

"You are a very bad boy…and just thought you needed punished!" I said with a smile.

"Oh…well baby you haven't seen my bad boy side yet!" as he kissed my lips.

As we lay there kissing he slowly entered me softly. I Started grabbing at his back the more he pumped me. Next thing I knew was the great pleasure that was rushing over me. We both began moaning the harder and faster our movements. Until finally our bodies Started going into orgasmic bliss as we both collapsed on each other.

~*~

CHAPTER SIX

We lay there gasping for air, as our heartbeats were calming down. Damian caressed my body as we lay in the bliss of the moment.

Next thing I knew Damian was making no movement. I looked over at him to see him sleeping away. As I looked at him I noticed how truly beautiful he really was. I ran my hand along his face and my fingers along his lips.

"Wow...you are truly amazing!" I whispered to myself.

As I looked him over to myself I was thinking how amazing it would be to wake up next to him every morning. I could remember thinking how I really could get used to him. I mean what's not to love about him. First his eyes were a deep blue truly beautiful. His lips big and full he could kiss very well. He was full of passion and compassion which is quite rare trust me I have extensive experience with the dating scene.

His body amazing, he was quite buff and gorgeous and his voice amazing. But could this man truly be for real could he really be the man that truly understands and love women the way he sings about.

I felt myself falling for him but me be tied down to one man only. I had been so successful in my life and I got this way by working hard and was I willing to blow my whole life on one man that for some reason I connected to on more than just a physical level. I quickly rolled over to face the wall. With everything in me I tried to get up out of bed but for some reason I couldn't. But I knew if I didn't it would be the start of my downfall in my life. I Started to get up when I felt him pull me into an embrace.

He rolled me over and pulled me into a passionate kiss. I couldn't resist him and I accepted his kiss.

He pulled back from my lips to look at me he smiled and ran his fingers through my long silky auburn hair. We just sat there looking at each other as our hands found the others.

"I could really get used to this!" he whispered as he kissed my lips.

"Yeah…me too!" I let slip out.

"Well I do have to say I'm quite starving now!" he laughed.

"I think we should take advantage of this room and order some room service…what do you think?" he asked with a smile.

I smiled as I grabbed the menu by the phone and gave it to him graciously. He took it and Started looking over it as I got up wrapping a sheet about my body and headed for the bathroom. In the middle of the room was a whirlpool bath, which was encased by beautiful candles that were a fresh flowery scent. The room was illuminated with the candles and self-dimming lights. I reached over the tub and turned on the facet to draw a bath and adding some bubble bath that was around the tub.

~*~

CHAPTER SEVEN

I let my sheet drop by the tub and stepped into the huge tub as the jets moved the bubbles around whilst relaxing my body. I laid my head against the back of the tub where I placed a bath pillow. I took in the scent of the candles as I slowly ran my fingers through my long blonde hair. I could feel the days' stresses washing away from me before I knew it I felt hands shaking me.

"Makayla…sweetie what do you want to eat?" I heard Damian asking me.

"What I said as I looked back at him sleepily.

"Oh just order what you got!" I smiled at him.

"Okay umm…please give us another order of the chicken pasta!" he said to the person over the phone.

He hung up and dropped his boxers in front of the tub.

"Can I join you…it looks really inviting!" he said with a cheeky smile.

"Yeah…sure!' I said as I rolled my eyes and moved out of the way.

"Hot…hot!" he said as he stepped in.

Damian finally got in and pulled me toward him. Where my ass rested on his cock.

"Umm…just the way I like it!" he whispered into my ear whilst kissing my neck.

"Mmm!" I whispered as I felt each kiss as it sent chills along my back.

He pulled me tighter into the embrace as I turned to meet his lips whilst touching and rubbing his quickly hard cock. I placed his hands upon my pussy as he inserted one of his fingers. He started circular motion as he inserted another. With every movement he enticed me all that much more. I began stroking him faster as the waves of ecstasy casted a spelled upon me.

"Put your pussy upon my cock!" he whispered softly in my ear whilst kissing my lips passionately.

As our moans filled the room I slowly turned around to grant his desire. I raised myself upon his hard cock and slowly let my pussy lips engulf him.

"Oh god…mm!" I said as I licked my lips.

"Oh yes!" he moaned as he held me tighter.

Soon our moans were ringing throughout the room the more we pleasured each other.

"Yes…yes!" he moaned as his lips met mine.

The water around us started splashing about the faster we moved as one. Finally, after a few minutes we both reached our orgasmic bliss. Most of our strength was gone as we collapsed in each other's arms.

"I can't breathe!" I whispered to him in his ear.

"Neither can I!" he said breathlessly.

I lay my head upon his shoulders to rest as he laid his on mine.

We sat there in silence holding and caressing each other.

After a few minutes there was a knock at the door.

"Oh man…I don't want to move!" he said with a smile.

We looked at each other. I gave Damian a kiss on his lips and I moved off him.

"Be right back!" I said with a smile as I placed my hand upon his cheek.

He took my hand and kissed it and held it until he couldn't anymore.

I placed a white terry cloth robe about my body and head for the door stealing one last look at the beauty looking at me. I opened the door to see room service looking back at me. I watched as the man wheeled the cart into the room and placed it by a dining table out on the balcony. I reached for my purse and grabbed a ten from it and handed it to the man as he was leaving the room.

~*~

CHAPTER EIGHT

I grabbed a glass of white wine as I stepped out on the balcony. I was standing there enjoying the breezes and scenery when Damian came up behind me wrapping his arms about my waist.

"Hey baby…I missed you!" he said whilst kissing my neck.

I turned to face Damian. We stood there looking at each other we didn't seem to need words to tell how the other one felt.

"I missed you too!" I said as I pulled Damian to me.

In that moment he held me so tightly and something about the way he held me felt so right.

"Shall we eat?" he asked as he placed a kiss on my lips.

"Yeah that would be great!" I said with a smile as our embraced broke.

Damian went over to the cart and lifted the lid to the entrees.

"Mmm…smells great!" as he inhaled the smell.

Damian motioned for me to sit as he placed the dinners in front of us.

"More wine sweets?" he asked.

"Please and thank you…Hun!" I said with a smile.

Damian poured himself a glass of wine and then lights the candles and took his seat.

We sat there eating and making small talk and then Damian gave me the run-down of everything he wanted out of a manger. Over dinner Damian would place his hand upon mine.

"So Makayla are you with anyone?" he asked interested.

"Umm…no god I would hope not with what we have done in the past couple hours. I said with a giggle.

"I'm sorry that was such a stupid question!" he chuckled nervously.

"So how is your music coming along…since the split?" I asked.

"It's coming on my second solo album!" he said as he sipped his wine.

"So why is it you aren't attached?" I asked with a wink.

"Just I guessed I haven't found anyone to share my life with!" he said sadly.

"I mean I would love to share my life with someone…I would love to be a Daddy!" he said.

"I tell you I love the success I have had but would trade it all gladly to be a husband and father…I'm so jealous of Layne…just to have someone to love would be a blessing in itself!" he said blinking back tears.

"I'm so lonely…nights are so long and cold!" he went on.

"Makayla…could you please stay the weekend with me…I so don't want to be alone!" he said as he grabbed my hand.

I choked on a piece of pasta I was eating when he asked me the question. But I saw the desperation in his face and maybe I was feeling kind of lonely and empty too.

"What…omg!" I coughed.

"Makayla…are you okay here have a drink of water!" he said anxiously.

I grabbed the glass of water he poured me and raised it to my lips.

"Thanks!" I said shyly.

"So will you stay the weekend with me?" he asked.

"I mean please this is really odd behavior out of me…but I don't sleep around…I would rather please myself then to sleep around…with all the diseases out there…but there is just something about you that intrigues me so much about you…I feel such a connection with you!" he said as he bent down in front of me.

As he looked up at me with his puppy dog eyes my heart almost broke for him. To me he sounded so pathetic but he was right there being something there and not to mention he really was easy and awesome to be with and was the most amazing lay. Who really could blame me he was so sexy and compassionate and we had such chemistry between us it was almost scary.

~*~

CHAPTER NINE

"Okay sure...I will stay!" I said with a smile.

"Omg...are you sure?" he asked.

"Never been more sure in my life!" I replied.

Damian was so happy he couldn't stand it and he swooped me up into his arms. As he carried me our gazes met and I got lost in his eyes. He placed his lips to mine our lips met and we started kissing each other passionately. I thought I heard Damian say he loved me as he lay me gently back on the bed. He pulled at the ties on my robe removing it exposing my naked body. He ran his hands along my body exploring every inch as if this was our first time being together. His lips met mine once more and we Started moving together as one again.

As the event went on I was more convinced that he was making love to me. This couldn't be possible we barely knew each other. I don't think we got out of bed the whole weekend until Monday morning. He got up and showered and dressed to get ready to leave. He ordered a car to bring us back to my office. The ride there was spent holding each other but very quiet and somber. Over the past weekend not only did we have amazing sex. I also got to know him a little better and I truly started connecting with him. But I was no sooner ready to get tied down to him then at the beginning of the weekend.

But I really do have to admit he had taught me how to feel a lot better. But I knew what was going to happen next and would I be strong enough to put my foot down. We walked into the building thank god no one was around to see us.

We walked into my office hand and hand here it comes the moment of truth.

"So I guess I need to get going!" he said with a hint of sadness.

"Yah!" I said still clinging to Damian.

"So umm where are you headed?" I asked him with a hint of sadness.

"I got to go to London!" he said as he ran his fingers through my hair.

"God…how I will miss you Makayla!" he said with a sad smile.

"When I get back…I would love to see you…first thing!" he said with a kiss.

"Well Damian…I really don't know!" I started to say when I saw the light in his eyes fade.

"Please Makayla… I believe I have falling for you!" he whispered.

With that I was frozen stiff I couldn't move let alone speak. Damian got a glimpse of his watch.

"Dam it…I have to go got a flight this afternoon…still have to pack!" he said as he Started kissing me passionately.

His kiss totally blew me away and all I wanted was to stay there in his arms. He finally pulled away as I stood there with my eyes closed waiting for his next kiss. He started to walk away when he stopped and pulled something out of his pocket. My heart almost skipped a bit when he called my name.

"Makayla...I got this for you at the gift shop at the hotel!" he said as he placed a small crystal cube in my hand with two hearts etched in the glass and the words I love you.

"Thank you...umm it's beautiful!" was all I said.

"Just something to remember me by!" he said sadly as he turned and walked on to the elevator. I knew those words will haunt me for the rest of my days.

CHAPTER TEN

I walked into my office and showered and changed into a pink cashmere pantsuit with a with white silky button down shirt underneath. I was done in the nick of time to see Cyndi taking a seat at her desk. I walked over to her to see her and gather any messages she had gotten from voicemail. As I walked closer I could see her on edge.

"What's the matter Cyndi?" I asked as I saw her hand handing a pen to her daughter.

"Omg…what have I told you about bringing your child to work?" I scolded her.

"Miss Weiss…please don't get mad …Dan will be coming to get her in a few minutes on his way back from working last night!" she said.

"Okay…this is an office and we don't need kids under feet!" I said as I walked back into my office.

"What is wrong with you girl…stop being such a bitch!" I said to myself as I looked out my window.

Just then I saw a couple fighting just outside my window. The man was just screaming at the lady beside him and I could see tears rolling down her cheeks.

I was taken back to a very abusive relationship in my past. *Grant was so abusive to me. I remember coming home from a long day at work from my own business and I heard noises coming from a back room of our house. I walked on further thinking I would see Grant watching TV or something. Yeah it was something alright! I saw Grant in bed with another woman. They were deeply into the act when I caught them. They were both moaning and screaming and it was my bed. I was so crushed. He saw me and got so furious with me as if I had some nerve begin there. I guess I must have interrupted. He came at me with full force he pushed me out of the bedroom and handcuff me to a table on the outside of our room where he left me and went back to the lady. They didn't emerge until hours later all the while I had to listen to them fucking and how he professes his love to that woman.*

After they were done she left and then he demanded that I cook him dinner and when I refused he beat the living hell out of me. He beat for the bad day he had he beat me because the cans and spices weren't alphabetized. Needless to tell I made it out of there via an ambulance. I was put in the hospital and I went to file a report against him and get an order of protection. It did me no good as he worked for the Police department. I remember looking like a fool because every one of those guys knew my fiancé was fucking around on me and they got their rocks off knowing what I didn't. Not to mention the one time he drugged me and let his friend have their way with me.

By the end of this I didn't have a business and I left with just my clothes on my back. I had to get away far away from him as I could. I was brought back to the present with the ringing of the phone.

I just let the phone ring and it went right over to the voicemail.

As the days past I found myself dodging Damian's phone calls at work and at my place. I really couldn't bring myself to talk to him. I even decided I couldn't be his manger either and I knew I had to tell him sooner or later. I listen to his messages all confessing his love for me but I couldn't go down that road again. I know he would most likely do the same thing as every other guy in the world.

CHAPTER ELEVEN

I woke to the blaring of my alarm clock. I untangled myself from my sheet and turned my alarm off. Through my blurred vision I saw man lying next to me in my bed.

"Get your lazy ass up…and get the hell out of here!" I hissed.

The guy looked at me like I was some crazy woman and grabbed his things and left just the way he came.

"Men!" I hissed as I walked into my bathroom.

I turned the water on and light the candles around the tub. After a few minutes the room was filling with the aroma of fresh flowers.

I slipped into the bubble bath wincing from the hotness of the water.

I leaned back resting against the bath pillow as I let the water rush over my body. Something about the way the bathroom felt brought me back to the weekend I spent with Damian. Parts of me missed him so much but I knew this couldn't work out. I closed my eyes and was on the brink of relaxing when the phone began ringing.

"God who is it now!" I said as I grabbed the towel from the back of the door.

As I walked out to my room I heard the machine pick up.

"Makayla Weiss…I'm not home you know the drill!"

"Makayla…ya I know the drill all too much…I know you are there it is Saturday…pick up…please!" Damian said.

"I miss you so much love…can you please talk to me…I mean what is your problem!" Damian went on.

This was nuts I needed just to end this right now. But part of me like having Damian calling me all the time but he did deserve me to talk to him.

"Hello!" I said as I grabbed the phone.

"Makayla…god how are you …I've been trying to call you all week!" he went on.

"So when can I see you again…I miss you so much…the weekend was amazing!" he continued.

"Damian please…I can't do this!" I said in a whisper.

"I can't be your manger!" I said to him.

"What Makayla…what about our weekend!" he said confused.

What about us!" he replied.

"Damian there is no us…there never will be…it was just a fuck session!" I yelled.

"You don't mean that…please tell me you take it back!"

"Damian …like I said it was just a fuck okay…get over it buddy…go on with your life!" I said so cold-heartedly.

With that I heard nothing more than a dial tone.

~*~

CHAPTER TWELVE

Since I spoke to Damian I had already set him up with another manger named David. I knew through the grape vine that Damian wasn't too happy about the manger I sent to him. Part of me was miserable without Damian but I couldn't give him what he needed and he deserved better too. He was such an amazing man but I knew he would eventually have turned back into a frog it was just a matter of time they all do. I went out a couple times with friends and with guys a girl needs to get her rocks off too. After work tonight I would be going over to Ashley's house to celebrate Jackie's 36th birthday. I hopped on a short flight to San Fran, as I would be spending the weekend with all of them. I entered the plane and quickly took my seat after an hour I was hailing a cab from the airport to Ashley's house. I paid the driver and got out and soon I rang the doorbell. I heard everyone call my name out as the door opened. Jackie greeted me as she threw her arms around me.

"Hey Mac long time no see!" she said with a smile.

"Omg…it's been way too long in fact!" I said as we walked together back inside the house.

I could tell Ashley was a little jealous as everyone's reaction to me.

"You are late!" Ashley informed me.

"I'm sorry but I do get to make a living too!" I hissed back at her.

We were starting to sing Happy birthday to Jackie as there was chaos all around. Children screaming and running about and untidiness all around.

I so couldn't figure why both my sister ever chose this path that was laid out in front of them. Screaming kids, changing diapers, carpool and PTA meetings. I so would not pick this live for me in a million years and besides I have way too much fun being me. I knew I would never find the right man mostly because he isn't out there to find.

After cake and ice cream my two sisters and I went into the kitchen and helped clean up the kitchen. As we cleaned up we were all cracking jokes well mostly Jackie and I. Ashley was always the boring one of the bunch but she was comfortable being that way. Next thing we brought coffee out to the guys as Jackie decided to put in a CD and grabbed my arm to join in and dance with her. Next thing I knew everyone was dancing around the room well everyone except Ashley.

Jackie and I were shaking like a leaf on a tree as we danced with the music. The night finally came to a close and I would be staying with Jackie and Jake only a couple houses away from Ashley. That night there was a knock at the door to the spare room I was staying in. KNOCK…KNOCK

"Yeah who is it?" I asked through the door.

"Aunt Mac it is Jenna!" I opened the door and let her entered my room and we took a seat on the bed.

"Look what I got!" she said with a laugh.

~*~

CHAPTER THIRTEEN

Jenna handed me what she wanted to show me.

"Wow…a fake id!" I said as I gave her a wink.

During the weekend I went with the family to movies and to dinner and cookouts. Before I knew it I was back home unlocking my front door to my big house in the hills. It was great being home again in my own domain. My home was so clean you could eat off the floor. I decided I would sit in my Jacuzzi. I needed to wind down before I returned to work the next day. I sat in the Jacuzzi taking in the sights of the bright lights of LA below. I got out of the Jacuzzi and wrapped my silky white robe around me and decided on a glass of white wine as I stood on my balcony while once again taking in the lights below.

I headed back into my room to shower and get ready for bed. I put on my silky cami short set and pulled back the blankets to get into bed.

I turned the side light off and pulled the covers up over me. For some reason tonight I Started tossing and turning. Maybe it was because I knew my sister Jackie and Jake left early that morning for a bed and breakfast somewhere in Napa Valley for Jake special birthday present to Jackie. They would be there for a week or so. I know I shouldn't worry what could really happen to them. My mind drifted to the awesome weekend that not too long ago I spent with Damian.

It had been a month or so since that day. Each day grew lonelier since I decided I wouldn't be able to be

Damian's manger. I rolled over and opened the drawer of the night table and pulled out the small crystal cube he had given me. Why did I decide to keep this gift? I should've thrown it away but I couldn't part with it.

"Dam it…why do I do this to myself!" I hissed as I threw the cube away in the garbage beside my bed.

Finally, I got him out of my mind near 6am and I was able to get a few winks before my alarm went off about 8am.

I woke to the blaring of my alarm and rolled over and turned it off.

I got up and headed in to take a shower when I stepped on something.

"Ouch fuck!" I cried out in pain.

I turned on the light where I saw a rainbow streaks across the bathroom. I picked it up to see it was the crystal cube thingy Damian had got me sitting right in the middle of the floor. I looked around to see my seal point Persian cat named Diamond sitting on the window seat looking outside. I thought to myself maybe she liked it dragged it out of the garbage.

I threw it on my bed and headed for the shower. After my shower I threw on a dress and a blazer to go over it. I checked my look in my mirror and headed out through my kitchen grabbing my travel mug filling it with my Starbucks coffee. But to my surprise the coffee maker wasn't turned on.

"Dam it…I so need a coffee this morning!" I said as I slammed my fist on the marble countertop.

I looked down at my watch and realized I still have some time and I would be able to swing by the nearest Starbucks on the way to the office.

~*~

CHAPTER FOURTEEN

I left my travel mug on the counter and went out the door leading to the garage via the kitchen.

"Of all the days for me not to remember last night to set my coffeemaker timer…fuck!" I hissed as I hit the unlock button on my Mercedes.

I threw my briefcase and purse on the passenger seat next to me. I turned the radio up and pushed the button to put the top down. As soon as I heard the first few notes of the song I knew it was Damian's music coming through my speakers. The music coming from the speakers was pretty soothing so I didn't bother to change the channel.

"Dam!" I hissed as I put my glasses on my face and backed out the driveway.

After a few minutes I pulled up at a Starbucks near the office. I put my car in park and turned it off and got out of the car. I was almost to the door when I realized I needed my purse I had left in the car. I turned around and walked back to my car and bent over the car door and reached for my purse but as I pulled it up to me it I dropped my wallet and checkbook and brush.

Unknown to me a dark haired man with a dark hair lady and a small baby walked past my car.

"Mmm…mm!" Damian said as he watched a lady bent over a car door.

"Nice ass!" Damian said as he held his hand over his heart.

"Dam Damian get your mind out of the gutter!" Layne hit Damian upside his head as they walked past.

"You are right…I'm still hoping I can convince Makayla to come back and maybe work on getting her to at least give us a chance again!" he said with sadness.

"Damian I really hope so for your sake…you really do care about her don't you?" Layne said as she placed her hand on his shoulders.

"Yeah I really do!" he said with sadness.

They walked into the Starbuck and ordered their coffees.

"Okay you let's give Mommy a moments rest!" Damian said as he took Calvin over to a table.

I walked into Starbucks as soon as I gathered my things and placed my order. As I waited I decided to take a bathroom break. I walked into the restroom and checked my look in the mirror as I put on my lipstick and sprayed some Spiced Green Tea on my neck and wrist. The room was filling up rather quickly and I made my way back to the counter still waiting for my latté. As I waited I looked around and then at my watch and my name was called and I made my way over the counter. As I grabbed my latte and made my way out in between the tables. As I looked straight ahead that is when I saw Damian sitting there with my best guess Layne. I came to a dead stop where I watched Damian playing with the baby.

~*~

CHAPTER FIFTEEN

Part of me was so excited to see him.

"Omg…could it be Damian?" I asked myself quietly.

"I so would love to talk to him again!"

"No …I can't!"

"He is an adult and so are you!" I mumbled to myself.

For a moment I could see Damian and me with a family and just enjoying each other's company. From the look of it Damian would so be an awesome Daddy. I so knew that Damian wanted that more than anything. I stood there smiling at the sight of him. I Started moving closer to him and had my hand extended out to tap him on his shoulder. Until Damian bent over to pick up the toys for the baby as Layne talked on the phone.

"No…I can't do this!" I said as I by passed Damian's table and headed for the exit.

Just as Damian was sitting back up he smelled a familiar scent.

"OMG…it can't be!" he said as he got up from the table to follow the scent like a faithful hound dog.

"Damian…where are you going?" Layne started to say as she watched Damian walk by as if he was in a trance.

"I'll be right back!" he said as he walked past Layne.

Layne was curious and she grabbed Calvin and started to follow Damian outside.

"Makayla!" he called as he saw the back of a long Auburn lady with curly hair a short dress gets into a red convertible Mercedes AMG.

I got into my car and placed my coffee in the holder.

"Oh god that was so close!" I said as I was backing out of the parking space.

"Makayla…dam wait!" he screamed as he kicked at the rocks and sand.

"Fuck me…dam it if only I was a few minutes earlier!" he said with such disappointment.

My heart was beating so hard it almost jumped out of my chest.

It was so great just to see Damian from a far today but I wonder what he is doing in LA maybe he lives here too. All I knew is I needed to get to work before I was late I so hated people that weren't punctual.

After a few minutes I was pulling up at the office and into my spot.

"What is wrong with you?" Layne asked a very upset Damian.

"Did you see her?" he asked.

"See who!" Layne said trying to follow him.

"Never mind can we go to that appointment?" he said as he walked back in.

"Sure I'm ready when you are!" she said with a smile.

Damian helped Layne gather up her things and grabbed his coffee and was headed toward the exit.

Damian walked over to the rental car he and Layne had rented and opened the doors and put the things in the backseat. Damian took the driver's seat as Layne put Calvin in his car seat. After a few minutes Damian was pulling up at an office building. Damian made his way through the parking lot where he was pulling up in a reserved space.

"Damian this spot says reserved!" Layne pointed out.

"Yeah I can see that!" he hissed at her.

"Dam Damian what is with the attitude all of a sudden?" she questioned him.

"Nothing sorry Layne!" he started to say as he looked over at the spot next to him where he saw a red Mercedes Benz AMG.

"Wow what a nice car!" he said admiring the car next to him.

Then his attention was drawn to the sign above it Reserved for Makayla Weiss

"I guess that was her!" he thought to himself.

Damian parked a couple spots away from Makayla's car.

"Let's do this!" Damian said to Lea with a wink.

"Okay could you get Calvin's stroller please?" she asked.

I walked off the elevator to see Cyndi sitting at her desk.

"Good morning…Miss Weiss!" she replied.

"Good morning hun!" I replied back to her.

"Here are your messages and thanks for yesterday with my daughter and all!"

"No problem...do me a favor and just tell everyone I have meetings all day!" I said with a wink and went into my office.

I sat down at my desk and took a deep breath. I started thinking about the close encounter with Damian a few minutes ago. I grabbed my coffee and looked out the window at the colored leaves that twist and turned and made their way to the ground. I was back to the time of Jackie and I raking the leaves when we were children. I sipped my latte`. I saw my sister and I jumping in the leaves just as soon as we gathered up the leaves. I was brought back into the present with the buzzing of my phone.

~*~

CHAPTER SIXTEEN

"Yes Cyndi what is it?" I answered.

"Umm…everyone is waiting for you in the board room!"

"Okay tell them I will be right there!" I said as I grabbed my power points presentation and walked out of my office.

As I made my way out of my office I walked right into a person.

"Pardon me sir!" I said looking down at the ground.

"Makayla!" I heard as the voice sounded familiar.

I looked up to see Damian standing in front of me.

"Damian!" I said hiding my excitement.

"I need to talk to you…can we go in your office!" he asked sounding very professional.

"Damian sorry I have a board meeting!" I said as I walked away from him and down a long hallway.

Next thing I knew was Damian was now standing in front of me.

"Damian did you not hear me…I said I have a very important board meeting now!" I hissed as I walked around him continued on down the hall where Damian pushed me up against a wall. In a sense his hands upon my arms and his chest next to mine turned me on.

"Damian take your hands off me!" I hissed.

"Funny you liked my hands all over you a little over a month ago!" he replied with a matter of fact look in his eyes.

"Damian just leave me alone…now I have a meeting to attend!" I said as I pushed him away from me.

I straighten my outfit as I continued on my way to the meeting.

"Fine!" he hissed as he turned and walked away.

"Fine!" I said as I placed my hand on the knob to turn it taking one last look at Damian walking away.

God how my heart sank as I watched him walking away and turn the corner.

"Sorry I'm late…I was in the middle of something!" I said as I started setting up for the presentation.

The meeting lasted for several hours afterwards I was sorting everything out. Meanwhile unknown to me Damian had waited and also told Layne to head back to the hotel to put Calvin down for a nap after feeding him. As I was putting things away in a cabinet Damian found his way to the boardroom.

"What the fuck!" I started to say as Damian pushed me up against the cabinet.

"Is that anyway to greet somebody that just waited hours to talk to you!" he said as he moved closer to my lips.

"Damian…umm!" I started to say as the heat between us radiated.

"Damian what!" he said as he ran his fingers along my red luscious lips.

With that Damian devourer my lips in his while his hands roamed my body.

"Oh god!" I muttered as I dropped the papers I was putting away.

"God how I have missed you!" he mumbled in between kisses as the papers scattered around us.

Damian pulled me into an embrace whilst backing me up toward the table.

"God me too!" I moaned as I followed his lead as wrapped my arms about him.

Damian laid me back against the table as I wrapped my legs about his waist.

"Tell me how you want me…and how you never want to be apart again!" he muttered.

Oh yes…I want you so much it hurts!" she cried.

Damian started tugging at my blazer as he dropped it to the floor.

"Oh my god…I can't do this!" I said as I pushed away from him.

"Dam it Kayla…don't do this to me again!" he said with tears in his eyes.

"Damian please I can't!" I said as I grabbed my blazer and ran into the hallway.

I ran out of the boardroom and into a janitor's closet to get away from him. I peeked out the door and watched him walk the hallway searching for me.

"Makayla…where are you?" he said as he came closer to the door.

I quietly shut the door as I broke down and cried I really wanted Damian so much. But I knew he deserved better than me and I couldn't be all that he wanted. It had been awhile when I finally stopped crying and I heard no sounds outside the closet.

~*~

CHAPTER SEVENTEEN

I peeked out of the closet and saw no one around and decided the coast was clear. I walked caution

 along the hallway and made it to my office. Once in my office I started gathering my things to leave as it was getting later and everyone since had gone. I grabbed my big overcoat and walked out of my office and over to the elevators. I took it down to the lobby and said goodnight to the guard and headed out towards my car.

I got in my car and started it and looked in my rear view mirror to see the bluest eyes looking back at me.

"Holy shit…Damian you scared the hell out of me!" I said as I turned around to the backseat.

"Surprised!" he asked.

"Yeah wait a minute how in the hell you get in my car…and how do you know this is my car anyway!" I asked him with shock.

"You know one day your pretty little car will get stolen if you …don't stop leaving your car unlocked!' he chuckled as he moved closer to me.

"Okay smart ass that answers the first question…but how did you know this was my car!" I said with a slight smile.

"Umm…that sign says so!" he said pointing to the sign.

I looked at the sign and I started laughing at how stupid I just looked.

"Oh my god is that a laugh!" he said as he moved in to kiss my lips.

"Yeah I guess that was…anyhow you need to get going!" I said as I opened the car door.

"So that is how it is going to be I missed my ride and I waited all day to talk to you and then you want to play hide and seek…you know what is wrong with you…you can't at least give me a ride back to my hotel!" he went on.

"Damian…I never asked you to come here today alright…what's wrong with me…you barge in here wanting to talk to me …and then you try to steal my car…and now it's what's my problem…I guess you don't have any issues!" I hissed.

"Kayla…I wasn't trying to steal your car…you left it open and I took a seat in the back…and I'm trying to steal your car!" he blurted out.

"Ooo…whatever…just get in the front seat okay!" I hissed.

"Thank you!" he said with a cheeky smile.

"Whatever…just where is your dam hotel!" I said with anger.

"Umm…I don't know!" he said with a smile as he moved closer to me.

"OMG…what is the name of it than?" I asked getting more pissed by the moment.

"I don't know that either…Layne made the reservations!" he informed me.

"You are kidding me right!" I looked at him with disgust.

"No I'm not!" he said with a smile.

"OMG…then call her then!" I hissed.

"Umm…okay!' he said as he felt around his body for his phone.

"Dam I forgot it in Calvin's diaper bag!" he said with a chuckle.

"This is so not happening!" I hissed.

"This better not be some kind of a joke!" I hissed at him.

I looked in my purse to grab my cell phone as I picked it up I saw my phone was dead.

"Fuck me!" I yelled as I threw my phone on the floorboard.

"What is wrong…can I really!' he said with a huge grin on his face.

~*~

CHAPTER EIGHTEEN

I rolled my eyes at him and backed out of the parking space as the top went down.

"I think your car is awesome!" he said trying to make small talk.

"Thanks…working does have its perks!" I said as I smiled at him.

"So where are we going?" he asked.

"I guess to my place so you can make that call!" I replied.

"Oh okay!" he said as he placed his hand on top of mine on the shifter.

After a few minutes we pulled on the winding street that took you up into the hills. Damian took in the sights all around him as we made our way through the streets.

After a few minutes we pulled into my driveway.

"This is your house?" he asked.

"It's quite beautiful!" he said with a smile.

"Thanks!" I said as I pulled into the garage.

"Your welcome!" he said as he placed his hand on my thigh.

"Here make yourself useful!" I said as I threw the briefcase in his lap.

"Oh fuck me!" he winced in pain as he held his balls in his hand.

"Omg I'm so sorry!" I said with panic in my voice.

"No problem!" he muttered as he got out of the car.

I grabbed my purse and shut my car door behind me.

"Are you sure you are okay?" I asked as I walked up to him.

"Yeah!" he said with tears welling up in his eyes.

I unlocked the door that lead into my kitchen and placed my keys on the key holder next to the door. Damian placed the briefcase down on the dining room table and took a seat on the couch.

"Can I get you a stiff drink!" I said with a smirk.

"Please!" he looked at me with horror.

I poured us a glass of vodka and orange juice and I handed to him as I took a seat next to him.

"Are you hungry! I asked with a smile.

"Umm…extremely!" he said as his voice slowly started to sound normal.

I walked into the kitchen and pulled out some marinated chicken breast and place them on a plate.

"I will be right back…I've got to change into something comfortable!" I said as I walked over to my bedroom off the huge living room.

Damian shook his head and started walking around the room. Damian decided to take a seat on the couch. From the couch Damian could see my reflection in a mirror changing into a pair of yoga pants and a mint green sweater.

Damian was enjoying the view as he sipped his drink.

"Oh god…I so want to have her again!" he thought to himself.

I walked back out into the living room and turned on soundscape on my digital cable box.

"Better!" I asked him as I sat next to him and grabbed the drink from his hands and took a sip.

"Yes …thank you Kayla!" he said as he watched my lips on his glass as he was swallowing harder.

I bent over in front of him to grab my candle lighter after lighting the candles on the table.

"I guess I will go light the grill!" I said as I walked out the French door that spanned the back side of the house and opened up into an enormous pool and patio.

Damian followed me out the door and stood next to the grill. Damian grabbed the lighter from my hand.

"Can I light your fire?" he asked as he moved closer to me.

"Sure!" I said as I swallowed really hard at nearness of him.

"I'll go get the chicken!" I said as I sashay back into the house.

When I got back outside Damian was taking over at the grill.

I gave him the chicken breast as he gave me a soft kiss on my lips.

"I'll get the rest made!" I said as I smiled at him.

I stood inside the door for a few minutes watching Damian as he was cooking. It was so nice to see him again and to spend some time with him.

I walked in the kitchen and fixed the rest of dinner and was about done when Damian came in to get a plate. I grabbed a plate for him and handed it to him with a smile. He walked back out and I sat the table for two.

~*~

CHAPTER NINETEEN

Damian brought the chicken to the table and place apiece on each of our plates.

"Thank you Kayla for this!" he said with a smile.

"Your welcome…I hope you enjoy it…you like another drink?" I asked him.

"Umm you better watch out…I might begin to think you are trying to get me drunk…and have your way with me!" he chuckled.

"Maybe I am!" I chuckled at him.

I got up to get us another drink in the kitchen and make my way back to the table.

"Thanks!" he said with a smile.

After dinner I got up to clear the table and clean the kitchen. Damian followed me into the kitchen and helped me clean up the kitchen. Damian swatted me with a towel and ran out of the kitchen to hide from me.

"You are so going to get it!" I said with a laugh.

I chased Damian throughout the house. Finally, I went out the door that leads onto the patio. Just as I got out there Damian was standing there laughing at me. I saw Damian next to the pool and I pushed him into it.

"Told you!" I laughed as I stood by the pool gloating.

My phone began ringing so I turned around to walk away when Damian made his move and pulled me in by my feet.

I let out a scream and looked so shocked that he did what he did.

"Ha…now who is the smart one!" he said as he laughed.

I turned around to get out of the pool just as Damian grabbed me and kissed the back of my neck. His hand on my body was so exhilarating and I turned to face him. We just stood there just lost in each other's eyes. I started shaking from the cold and Damian pulled me into his arms to warm me.

"I'm sorry!" he whispered in my ears.

"It's okay!" I said with a smile still looking in his eyes.

Damian moved into me closer and wrapped his arms about me. I loved the way his arms felt around me and I moved in closer. Damian engulfed my lips and soon I was lost in him again. My heartbeat was echoing in my brain it was beating so fast. I started kissing him back with so much passion and urgency.

I quickly pulled away as it was starting to feel too good as I stood on the threshold of a raging storm within me.

"OMG I'm so stupid…oh god I can't do this!" I said aloud.

"What in the hell am I doing…this can't happen!" I said as I pulled myself from the pool.

"Why are you trying to complicate your life!" I said

"As if it isn't complicated enough!" As Damian looked over at me strangely.

"You know pull your head out of your ass…and use your brain girl!" I hissed still ranting whilst thinking aloud.

"Excuse me my head is not up my ass!" he said confused.

"What oh no I wasn't talking to you?" I said with a smile.

"Well it is not like anyone else is here but us!" he said looking at her strangely.

"I'm talking to myself dumbass!" I said harshly.

"Whom are you calling a dumb ass?" he replied.

"Dumbass, you are talking and answering yourself!" he said as he got out of the pool moving towards me.

"Ooooh…well I may be talking to myself…it's only because you drive me crazy!" I said as I watched him move closer as I was swallowing harder and my heart was beating like a drum.

"Well you drive me crazy too!" he said with his face nearing mine.

"So I drive you crazy …so I suppose I could kiss you and that would make you crazy too!" he replied as he pushed me closer to the French doors.

"I think you got this all wrong…I never said you drove me crazy!" I said still standing my ground as my body ached to be in his arms.

"Oh really!" he said with a smile.

"Yes Damian…oh really don't you know you are a little boy…that is so much fun to play with!" I said still trying to remain confident.

"So all I'am is just a toy to you!" he replied trying to act wounded.

"Well not really at least when I play with my Ken doll he doesn't give attitude!" I quickly defended.

"Attitude… I don't have an attitude!" he said.

"Damian you are a drama queen with a nice ass; but that is where it ends!" I came back.

"Hey now I'm more than just a nice ass and a pretty voice!" he went on.

"Umm…not really!" I replied. While my back rested on the glass door.

"Okay what about my hair…you like running your fingers through…or my engaging blue eyes…and my amazing smile and full lips!" he said as his nose rested on mine as I was swallowing harder and harder with each word he spoke.

"What…what about them?" I said growing hotter by the moment with only mill inches between us.

"You would miss them if they went away!" he said as he engulfed my lips.

~*~

CHAPTER TWENTY

As he kissed me my inhibitions were running rampant. Next thing I knew I was pulling him in towards me.

"Oh god I want you!" I said in between kisses.

With that Damian picked me up and I wrapped my legs about him as I thrusted my tongue into his mouth as he found his way to my bedroom. Finally, we made our way into the bedroom where he put me back on my feet as I started pulling at his t-shirt slowly pulling above his head exposing his blonde hairy chest as I placed baby kisses along his torso feeling his body twitching under my soft lips. My fingers started unbuckling his belt pulling it free from his waist. I then unbuttoned his pant button quickly arousing his once soft member.

"Oh god Kayla!" he moaned as he pushed my head down letting me know to go further.

I slowly pulled his pants down to his ankles and he kicked them off as he pulled me up to his mouth and kissed me passionately. Damian ran his hands along my silky arms and pulled my sweater up over my head exposing my full breast as he ran his finger along the border of my lacy bra. He then started kissing them softly as he slipped one strap off and then the next unbuttoning the strap letting it fall to the ground.

He then sucked at my breast as if he was a baby sucking mommy's milk taking his fill and then some.

"Ooh god yes!" I moaned.

He then pushed my pants down to my ankles as he pushed me backwards towards my bed. He then pulled himself over me until there was nothing left to see. He then devoured my lips as his tongue roamed my mouth as he touched my body sensually. He then started moving his hand up and down my thigh.

"God you are so beautiful baby!" he mumbled as his ran his fingers along my jaw line.

"God so are you…baby!" I whispered into his ear as I then proceeded to engulf his lips once more.

Damian ran his soft fingers along my torso and down towards my softness. As he kissed me he put his fingers into my panties and slowly pulled them off me and threw them down towards the ground. As he went back to rubbing his hands and fingers along my soft skin.

With a swift movement Damian slowly entered me, as we slowly started moving as one. Just for a moment time sieges as the two lovers surrender sweetly in each other's arms.

~*~

CHAPTER TWENTY-ONE

I devoured Damian's lips once more as my breathing was in time with Damian as our bodies just seem to blend and mesh in perfect harmony.

Even at this stage of events I couldn't deny my true feelings for him. I was falling faster and harder than I ever wanted too. So I felt as if I should just explore what I felt for him. What was I so afraid of him earlier? In this moment he had so much passion and he gave it so freely and with so much love. A woman could get used to feeling even for a moment feel important and that you were special to just one person.

Faster and faster our breathing became as we burned and ache for our deepest desire to engulf us and send the pleasure barreling through our bodies. Just as sure as the sun setting over LA Damian and I reached our orgasmic bliss. As we collapsed upon one another gasping for our next breath to speed its way to us.

"Oh god I can't breathe!" I gasped as my body came to rest right upon Damian's chest.

I listened as Damian speaking the same words as he kissed me on my cheek. I grabbed a hold of Damian so tightly as I didn't want to let him go. I laid there in the dark as Damian rolled over and cradled my body and pull it in to his. He started caressing me like no one else ever had and I knew I wanted to stay in this moment in time forever. The one thing that was left was if Damian really felt what he said he felt for me. Or had I push him to far away from us. I once again laid there in his arms never wanting to move or wake up the connection that was between us. We both fell asleep in the arms of one another. I remember waking to the sound of a ringing cell phone.

I slowly moved Damian's arms off me and got up and started searching around for what was the source of the ringing. It stopped ringing just as I got up to where our clothing lay in a pile in the middle of my bedroom floor. Then the phone started ringing again and I finally found it in one of Damian's jacket pockets. As the phone rang in my hand I read a name of a girl and I quickly opened the lines.

"Hi baby…how are you doing and when are you coming back home?"

"Excuse me…who are you?" I asked as a lump started forming in my throat.

"Excuse you…who the hell do you think you are…omg you spent the night with Damian!" she spat out.

"Umm… that depends on who wants to know?" I hissed as Damian started stirring.

"Well I'm his girlfriend Beth!" she said again.

"What…Damian isn't with anyone…at least that is what he informed me!" I asked feeling pangs of hurt in my chest as I took a seat on the edge of my bed.

"Yeah…then who am I then and we are expecting a baby next year!" she said as I couldn't bear anymore and I dropped the phone to the ground. I started crying silently and staring into space as the pangs of hurt coursed through my veins. I knew I was ready to give my all to Damian but I guess he is just like all the other guys in the world. My world was started crumbling around me and soon I was licking my scratches. Why did he claim not to have his cell phone when he did? He lied one lie after another and my trust for him was fading just as the night giving way to the morning light.

I felt my bed moving as Damian sat up in the bed and put his arms around me. I quickly pulled away from him as I got up and went over to his phone hurling it at Damian.

"You lied to me!" I said as tears ran down my cheeks.

"You had your phone all along…you tricked me!" I hissed at him throwing a vase in his direction.

"Kayla…I'm sorry I just wanted to see you again and have you come to work for me!" he said moving closer to me.

"Stop it don't call me that!" I cried.

"Kayla…I love you and I was hoping you would reconsider and give our love a chance!" he said as tears started welling up in his eyes.

"Stop don't you call me that!" I said as I covered my ears.

I had my back towards Damian as he came up behind me and starting leaving a trail of kisses along my neck.

Just for a moment I let him in and I enjoyed the closeness of us.

"You feel that Kayla…my heart races when you are around!" he said as he put my hand on his heart.

"Oh no Damian you are a heartless prick!" I hissed pushing away from him.

"Let me guess you feel like this towards Beth!" I hissed.

"What omg!" he started laughing.

"Beth!" he laughed again.

"Yes you are going to be a father next year!" I repeated what she said.

"No I'm not…you want to know about Beth…I just went out with her to make Layne happy!" he said with a laugh.

"I so didn't like that girl…I couldn't stand her being around me!" he said with the look of his skin crawling.

"Okay explain to me…how I can be a dad if I never had sexual relations with her…I told you before I just don't sleep around!" he exclaimed.

"Oh please save that for Beth!" I hissed at him.

"What omg…gross!" he exclaimed.

"You know to think I wanted things to work out between us...Oh god I hate you…how could you do this to me!" I cried as my tears fell like the rain outside the window.

"Please Kayla…what are you saying…you can't be serious!" he said as he ran his fingers through his dark hair.

"Damian I am as serious as a heart attack…Just being with you sexually isn't enough for me anymore!" I cried as I walked over to the window.

"I want a us dam it!" I cried not turning away from the window.

As I stood there crying Damian was thinking about what I was saying and to my surprise he made a decision.

"Oh my god…what have I gotten myself into…I stood there lying over and over at Kayla…The truth was that that night with Beth there was certain things Makayla shouldn't and can't know about…I was with Beth that night and I did sleep with her…but I was so drunk I barely remember it…and the truth was that we did have unprotected sex!" Damian was thinking this while I was crying.

"As much as I wanted Kayla I couldn't drag her through this if she knew the truth…Kayla would surely leave me…so as much as this hurts until I can get a paternity test done I can't let Kayla in my world…god why now when she was ready to be with me…do I get into such a huge mess!" he thought.

~*~

CHAPTER TWENTY-TWO

"You want an us now, what in the last 12 hours has he changed your mine about us!" he hissed.

"Remember 12 hours I was nothing but a Ken doll with a nice ass!" He went on.

"I had absolutely no effect on you what so ever!" He went on.

"I was nothing my engaging eyes, nice soft lips had no effect on you!" He said as he turned towards the window.

"Well maybe I was scare or maybe I was lying, but I couldn't bear to be hurt by a man again…I've been so hurt many times before!" I said as my tears fell down my cheeks.

"What I think you need is to take some time and think about that because I don't think 12 hours is long enough to change ones mine…Because it will take me longer to get over the awful things you have said!" he spat out.

With that Damian started gathering his clothes and went into the bathroom and I heard the shower turn on. After a few minutes there was a knock at my front door. I put my robe on and headed for the front door meanwhile Damian came in from the room and headed right over to the door and answered it before I could. Within a few minutes

Damian had followed the dark hair lady with a baby out my front door leaving me with just my thoughts.

I slid down the door crying as I put my head in my hands and stayed there for a while. The sun started coming through the blinds and the silence in the room was disrupted with the ringing of my house phone.

It rang a few times before I made it to my feet and stumbled over to my phone. My heart started racing as I let out my breath and grabbed the handle of the phone.

"Hello!" I said sniffling.

"Makayla!" I heard a very distraught Ashley on the other end.

"Ashley…what's the matter?" I asked starting to feel butterflies in my belly.

"Oh god I can't do this again!" she whispered as she broke down again.

"Ashley what is the matter…do what again…you are scaring me please tell me!" I said on the brink of tears.

"Okay…umm Makayla…it's Jackie and Jake!" she started to say.

"What about them talk to me you are scaring me!" I said impatiently.

"Oh…god Makayla…Jackie and Jake was in a bad car wreck on the way back from Napa!"

"What omg…please tell me they are alright!" I listen intently.

"Oh god Mac…they are dead!" she broke out and sobbed uncontrollably.

"What!" was all I could say as my sobs overcame me.

"Oh god no!" I cried aloud.

"Not Jackie!" I cried.

"OMG…I'm on the next flight!" I said as I hung up.

As I put the phone down I started completely breaking down as I tried to reach for my phone book.

"Oh god no this can't be happening!" I cried as I flipped through the pages to the airlines.

"Why Jackie…god no!" I said as my head started pounding as I dropped the book off the counter.

"No not Jackie!" I cried as I threw the phone across the room.

I fell to the floor sobbing uncontrollably as I put my head in my hands as I rocked back and forth.

After a few minutes I started thinking about my nieces and nephews. I crawled over to my phone and my book and held my tears inside as best I could and made my reservations. I got to my feet and ran into my bedroom and fell against my bed where I started crying profusely.

"Oh poor Jenna and Ben and Meghan…what will come of them?" I cried profusely.

"Those poor babies just lost their Mom and Daddy!" I cried aloud.

"My Jackie…how will I go on without you!" I cried.

But my thoughts were put on the back burner for now as I thought of those babies and I realized right I needed to be strong for them. So I dried my eyes and grabbed my suitcase from the closet and started throwing my belongings in it. As I quickly jumped into the shower and dressed before I needed to head for the airport for my flight.

~*~

CHAPTER TWENTY-THREE

I got to the terminal in just enough time to board the plane. I took my seat in first class in record time. Not long after we were taxing down the runway. I sat there looking out the window with the world on my shoulders. I mostly was hurting because it was too hard to accept that I would never see my sister ever again. It hurt me to know that those babies didn't have their parents anymore. How will they handle this or will they ever know just how great their parents truly were? And understand why god took their parents from them at such tender ages. Soon my pangs of sorrow consumed me and overwhelmed me all at the same time. I silently sat in my seat-crying river of tears through my swollen eyes.

My attention was captured by the cries of a baby, which just kick me into full gear. My heart was slowly breaking in two as if my sister's death wasn't enough. There was Damian also and my feelings I had to deal with to. What was it doing god just not like me at this moment in time. Have I really been that bad in my life that god had to punish me for some reason or another?

I glanced around the cabin and saw a woman crying she seem so distraught that my heart was breaking for her when I realized it was Makayla. My heart ache that much more that I wanted to go over and hold her and take her pain from her. It pained me that I was most likely the cause of hers. I knew she couldn't see me but I was horrified that she would if Calvin didn't stop his crying.

Then I realized that she seems to be crying in unison with Calvin. I turned back towards the window. I felt like such a shit for hurting Kayla the way I did and how I left her with the burdens of mine. But I couldn't drag Kayla through the pain that Beth would bring to us sooner or later. I was hoping to be able to come back at a later date to tell Kayla exactly why I did what I did to her. Hopefully she loves me enough to let me back in. God how I hated myself and Beth for what mess I have found myself in.

Please forgive me Kayla for doing what I did. I know you didn't mean what you have said. I knew you were only speaking from past hurts you have gone through lord knows I have had my fair share too. I so love you Kayla and I hated what I had to do and say to you. But I know now I truly love you cause all I want to do is to protect you and keep you safe cause only the lord knows how crazy Beth has been and what she was capable of.

~*~

CHAPTER TWENTY-FOUR

The plane ride lasted for what it seems was eternity. I step out into the aisle and grabbed for my carry on in the compartment above my head. I was dreading what was waiting for me at the gate. I took a deep breath and continued on towards the exit door. Layne was about to get up right as the seat belt light went off and I pulled her back in the seat and told her to wait a few and it bothered her at first until she started looking in the same direction as me and noticed Makayla standing up. Her tears still seem to fall down her face and it pained me so. But I made it this far and I wasn't strong enough to stand before her again and repeat all the cruel things I shouldn't have said in the first place.

"Just looking at her hurts me so much Layne!" he said on the brink of tears.

"Damian I know how hard this has to be…but either lose Makayla for a few months or lose her for forever…the choice is yours!" she said to him as she patted him on his shoulder.

"Wouldn't you know Calvin would fall asleep now…instead of during the flight!" she said.

"Yeah but he is awesome Lea!" he said with a smile.

I finally exited the plane and through my burry vision I made my way to the gate. I slowly looked around to see Ashley's husband standing there waiting for me. I made my way over to him as soon as I was in striking distant from him he engulfed me in a hug.

"I'm so sorry Hun…I know how close especially you were to Jackie!" he said as he held me tightly.

"Thank you…but I can't believe Jackie and Jake is gone!" I cried.

"I know…it just seems like yesterday they were dropping the kids off to us for the week…and we just talked to them last night!" he whispered as he took my bag and we made our way over to baggage claim.

I followed him in silence and waited for the first sight of my bags. I quickly found them and was about to leave the area when a baby toy fell at my feet. I bent down without looking up and grabbed the toy.

I came back up and handed it to the baby that a man was holding.

"Thanks mate!" he said as he turned to walk away.

"Your welcome!" I said as I continued to walk away when it dawns on me the scent the man was wearing and the sound of his familiar voice.

"Omg Damian!" I said as I turned to look but lost the sight of them in the crowd.

"Could it be…no!" I answered myself before I even could think twice.

We made our way through the crowd and out to the parking garage.

Teddy hit the button for the back of his SUV and started putting my bags into the back as I made my way up to the front passenger seat. As I stood there I started looking around to see a couple making their way to their car.

"God how I have missed you two!" I heard a man say as he pulled his wife and son into him.

"Me too!" she said as she kissed her hubby's cheek.

I was brought back into reality when Teddy opened the door for me. I quickly got in and grabbed a Kleenex from the box sitting on the dash.

I blew my nose as I stared into space and caught a glimpse of the same couple except I was staring into a familiar face. I was in shock to see Damian looking back at me from a back seat of the car in front of us. I stood there motionless as his smile faded to sadness as he reluctantly waved at me just as Teddy was backing away from the space. I almost waved back when the pangs of pain from the loss of my sister grabbed a hold of me once more. I started crying profusely again as Teddy reached over and patted my back.

"God I'm so sorry!" he said.

"Umm Ashley has been on the phone all day making the arrangements!" he shared with me.

That just sent waves of agony through me once more.

"Umm…I got to go to the morgue…you know to identified them!" he shared with me again.

"I'd thought it would be easier…rather then you and Ashley to do it!" he said as we drove on.

Within a matter of minutes, we were pulling up at the morgue.

"Umm…maybe it should be me to do that!" I commented to Teddy.

"Aw Hun are you sure?" he asked me.

"Yes!" I whispered quietly.

I reluctantly followed behind Teddy and into the morgue to identified them. Teddy informed the person behind the desk what we were there for. We were told to take a seat and someone would be with us in a moment. After a few we were called back and we were standing just outside the door. My heart was racing and I started feeling faint and took a deep breath and was just about to place my hand on the knob.

"I...I can't do this!" I cried as I took off in the opposite direction.

I rushed outside and took a seat on the steps and cried harder than ever before. My whole body started shaking like a leaf, as my breath seems to shorten.

After a few minutes the person behind the desk interrupted me.

"I'm sorry Miss but we can't let your brother –in-law do it!" he replied.

"What!" I said blankly back to that person.

"I'm sorry Hun...they won't let me!" Teddy said with regret.

I took one last deep breath and followed everyone inside and over to the bodies. I took a quick look and instantly knew it was Jackie and Jake.

"I'm so sorry!" the person replied as he handed me a big envelope.

I dropped the bag to the ground as I covered my face and sobbed.

I knew deep inside it was their belongings and I grabbed it and left the room to sign some papers. After that I went out to the car. The remainder of the ride back to Ashley and Teddy's was a somber one.

As Teddy pulled up he turned the car off and got out and started grabbing my bags from the back as I clutched the envelope and sat there crying. After a few minutes Ashley was at my door and engulfed me in a hug. The rest of the evening went by in a fog until we got to the party after the funerals.

~*~

CHAPTER TWENTY-FIVE

I couldn't bear anyone else to say how sorry they were for us. I broke from the party that Ashley had at Jackie and Jake's house and found my way upstairs and into Jackie's room. I started walking around aimlessly. I first grabbed my sister's perfume she always wore and smelled it. I inhale the fragrance as my tears immediately started falling as the scent made different memories come back to me. I was drawn to a picture of Jackie and Jake on one of the many trips they had taken over the years.

God how I missed them so much. I heard noises in my sister's closet and I slowly made it over to the door that was cracked opened a bit. I opened it to see Jenna, Ben and Meghan sitting amongst the clothing crying for their parents. My heart instantly broke for them as I took a seat next to them and put Meghan on my lap as each one said how much they missed their mom and dad.

"I know sweetie...I do too!" I said as we all grieved for them.

I sat there staring into space running my finger through Meghan's long hair. After a few minutes the door opened to reveal Ashley standing before us.

"Guys you all need to come downstairs...there are a lot of people here to give you their condolences!" she said.

With that I encouraged them to go downstairs after they left Ashley had something to ask me.

"Makayla...I need you to go to the store and get me blue napkins!" she exclaimed.

"Why not use the white ones downstairs?" I said blankly.

"What…I can't use them they don't match!" she hissed.

"You know I made all the arrangements…and did this and that and you can't be bothered…I don't want our Jackie's and Jake's to be remembered like that!" she hissed at me.

"Okay I'll go get them!" I said still crying from earlier.

I grabbed my purse and made my way to the corner store and grabbed the blue napkins Ashley requested. Later that night after everyone left I helped get the kids tucked in. A couple days later our sister's attorney needed to read our Jackie and Jake's will to us. I sat at the table just staring blankly out the window waiting for the attorney to begin. They went through everything and then the attorney was ready to tell us about the kids.

"Umm…okay the guardian of the children!" he started to say as he took a sip of water.

Ashley and myself were hanging on every word he was saying to us.

"Okay the guardianship of the kids goes to Makayla Weiss!" he replied.

When he said that I was in shock.

"What…Ashley should have them…she is the mommy type not me!" I quickly replied.

"What do you mean Makayla gets the kids…are you sure you are reading that right?" Ashley asked.

"Umm...I'm positive…Jackie wanted Makayla to have the kids!" he said handing over the papers.

"Umm…Jackie knew you all would react like this…so she left you both these!" the other attorney said as she hands us each a letter to read from Jackie.

"What?" I said as I got up from the table and stood by the window debating whether or not to read the letter I was now holding in my hands.

~*~

CHAPTER TWENTY-SIX

Makayla,

I am sure both you and Ashley are sitting there wondering why I did what I did. Why did I choose you for my kids? Well the answer is simple really. First off Ashley has her own family and does not need the burden of raising my kids. I know she would say it would not be a burden but you and I know better. The second reason, you need to settle down before you kill yourself. I can't think of a better reason to settle down than your sister's kids. They love you and you love them. And finally the third and most important reason why I chose you...I can only imagine you sitting on the edge of your seat right now waiting for me to just get to it...I know you all too well. The reason is, remember back in college, we went to that Halloween party and we dressed up like pregnant women. Ashley thought we were nuts, but we knew better. I remember seeing how proud you were of that belly, even if it was a fake belly. Makayla, you are going to make a great mother. You just have to believe in yourself. And if it helps know that I believe in you. My kids need you; they need your love and patience. They need your financial assistance. But most of all they need your free spirit. I hope this helps you to understand my decision. I love you Makayla now go and love my children. They are so easy to love.

Love always,

Jackie

Ashley,

*Wow, look at us now...all grown up and raising families of
our own. That is my reason for doing what I have done.
You have your own family. You don't need mine. Put your
trust in Makayla, she is going to need your help. Please be
there for her. I know you might say that Makayla and I are
far from grown up, but we are...We just have free spirits...I
want my kids to have them as well. Please understand that.
I did not make this choice to hurt you, I would never do
that. I love you...But I had to do what I thought was right
for my kids, and this is right. I also am doing this for
Makayla...I know you know what I am talking about when I
say that. Be there for her Ashley, please. Continue to love
her and continue to be family. For me! I love you so much.
Just please love each other.*

Love always,

Jackie

~*~

CHAPTER TWENTY-SEVEN

"Ring…Ring!"

Beth ran over to answer her phone.

"Hello!" she answered.

"Beth what the heck are you doing calling me?" he hissed.

"Damian I…I just wanted to talk to you!" she answered

"Well I told you I have nothing to talk to you about…until that baby is born and I prove it once and for all it is not my baby!" he hissed.

As Damian talked to Beth she went into a daze. She started having a flashback to the night of the date her and Damian went out.

She was taken back to dinner that night. They had gone out to an Italian restaurant. I watched as Damian drank several bottles of wine that night. Damian barely spoke any words to me just making small talk nothing to write home about.

One of my Uncle's was a pretty high up executive for Sony. I guess that was the only reason for him to date me. I guess just to score brownie points. Damian drove me back to my place where I invited him in. We started kissed and things started getting hot and heavy and I thought it was going somewhere so I went into my bathroom to put in my diaphragm. I returned a few minutes later to see a half-naked Damian in my bed but by this time he had passed out from the drinks.

I was so pissed that he fell asleep so I decided to finish undressing him the rest of the way and I took my clothes off and lay down next to him. When he woke the next morning he was horrified that we did something. Well at least that is what I wanted him to think.

My long-term boyfriend had broken up a few days prior. Shortly after Damian and I and we got back together and we end up making love. But I still have not forgiven my boyfriend for sleeping with some ho. I ended up catching him doing the deed and I was so pissed and hurt. I just wanted him to feel just an inkling of what I felt.

"Beth are listening to me!" I was brought back to reality.

"Yes Damian...sorry I was in my own world for a minute!" she said to him.

"Beth...I mean it stay the hell away from me!" he screamed.

"Yeah...yeah whatever...I thought you loved me!" she exclaimed.

"Don't you ever call me again...you got that!" he hissed.

"But we are having a baby...don't you want to see how your baby is coming along?" she cried.

"No!" he said as he hung up the phone.

~*~

CHAPTER TWENTY-EIGHT

After the meeting with the attorney we went back to Ashley's house. The ride there was a somber one I didn't know where to start first or the first thing about being a Mom. But somehow Jackie's letter put a little of my fears to rest. But I was so scared, what do I do now?

As we walked into the house Ashley automatically went up to her room. I could tell all that had transpired over the last couple hours hurt her.

"Aunt Mac…what happened?" the three kids all said in unison.

I knew I had to tell them all that had happened.

"Come and sit down!" I said to all of them with a smile.

"First off…well you all will be coming to live with me!"

"Really…cool!" they replied.

"Secondly umm…I need to know where do you all want to live?"

I waited for a while for an answer when they all reached a decision.

"Do we have to live in that house?"

"Umm…sweeties if you all want to then we can!"

"No!" Jenna replied.

"No!" Ben replied.

"Me either!" Meghan started crying.

"I kind of want to stay around here!" Jenna said.

"Me too!" Meghan cried as I held her close to me.

"Yeah...I do too!" Ben replied.

"Okay...well we can sell your house and put all the monies in trust for you all...and I guess with the sale of my home in LA...I could buy something close around here...and we can make a fresh start!" I replied as I looked at them.

"Okay just we got to go to LA and pack my house up so I can move here!" I said with hesitations.

"Seems how it's summer now and you all are on vacation...we all can go to LA and I can tie up my lose ends!"

"Yay!" they all said.

"Can we go outside and play Auntie Mac?" Meghan asked.

"Sure you all can go!" I replied.

They all went outside as I put my head in my hands and let out a big sigh.

"Oh god how am I going to do this?" I cried.

"Oh boy I hope I'm not making a big mistake!" I whispered as I poured me a cup of iced tea.

I watched the kids swinging on the swing in the back yard when Ashley walked in the room.

"So what are you doing...did you tell them?" she asked.

"Yes I did!" I said still looking out the window.

"And what?" she asked.

"Well I guess I will be looking at real estate now!" I replied.

"What you can't move them away...from all they know!" she hissed.

"What...this is what they want...they don't want to go back to their house...so I will find another one around here!" I replied.

"You can't do that!" she insisted.

"Ashley I think that is a great idea!" Teddy said from the doorway.

"What?" she hissed at him.

"She needs to keep them in their old house!" Ashley hissed.

"Ashley...I think Mac is doing the right thing...after all it is her responsibility now!" he said.

"Oh god help us!" she hissed as she left the room.

"No matter what I can never do anything right in her eyes!" I cried as I turned towards the window.

"I know...don't worry about her...I think you are doing right by them...so I guess you will be going back home to get everything prepared to sell?" he asked.

"Yeah for a few...seems how they are on vacation!" I said as I looked over at Teddy.

"I need to make some reservations!" I said as I went up to the guest room.

We would be leaving in a few days for LA. I woke up early the next day to start packing up Jackie's house and grab some of the kid's things to take to LA and pack up the rest to put in storage along with some of their parent's belongings they wanted to keep. It took me all day and half of the next day to finished up. On our way back to Ashley's I took the kids for pizza as it was getting late and they needed to eat and then go home and shower as we had an early flight the next am.

~*~

CHAPTER TWENTY-NINE

A few weeks had passed and I got many offers on my home in LA.

My staff was being pretty supportive of me and I relocated the main headquarters to the office in San Francisco. The kids and I spent a few weekends in San Francisco and even took in some sights and even looked at some houses in a small town called Sausalito. As we drove along the streets we saw some houses but was drawn to one in particular so we made an appointment to see this house. Instantly we fell in love with it and I put a bid in on the property. The house was perfect and so were the surrounding homes with a perfect view of the bay.

After a few weeks there was also bids on Jackie's house everything was going along smoothly. A month and a half before school we moved into the house. We were all excited and slowly getting back to normal well as normal as anything. I still missed my sister like crazy and I was still taking it pretty hard.

"Here we are!" I said as we drove up the driveway in a moving truck.

The kids could barely contain their enthusiasm and they all flew out of the SUV and onto the front porch.

"Okay here we go!" I said as I unlocked the front door.

We walked inside and I stood in the middle of the room to look around me as the kids went up and picked out their rooms. After I took it all in I walked outside and watched the Mover's opened up the moving truck.

I started taking boxes inside and putting them in the rightful rooms.

"Okay…I need all of your help please!" I called out.

One by one the kids made their way outside and started taking the boxes inside. I started putting away some of the boxes in the kitchen when Meghan came in and told me about a man outside who wanted to introduced himself.

"Come on Aunt Kayla!" she said as she dragged me outside.

When I got outside I saw a man had joined the team of the mover's and my helpers.

I also grabbed a dresser drawer and walked inside but I lost a few things.

"Hello!" he started to say while picking up some of my less flattering panties.

"Kayla OMG…you live here?" he asked still holding my panties.

"Yeah…I live here now…but what do you care for anyhow…don't you have something else to do besides bothering me!" I hissed as I turned back towards my house.

I walked ahead and on in my house as Damian followed me upstairs to my room.

"Kayla last I checked you didn't wear panties like this before!" he said as he held up my panties.

"Damian get the heck out of here okay…gees if I knew you lived around here I wouldn't have moved here!" I hissed as I yanked the panties from his hand and threw them on my bed.

"Well I guess we are neighbors!" he said as he pointed to his house you could see from my bedroom window.

"Just wonderful!" I said as I sat down on my bed.

"Kayla you look so tired Hun…can I do anything for you!" he said as he crouched down in front of me.

"No I wouldn't take your help if you were the last man on earth!" I said as I got up.

"Ouch that hurt!" he said as he looked up at me.

"You deserved it!" I hissed at him as I walked downstairs into my kitchen.

"Kayla please can we just talk!" he asked.

"No, Damian as a matter of fact I would like it if you would leave me the hell alone…it's too late for talk!" I hissed and continued unpacking my boxes.

With that Damian was about to turn and leave when I just had to ask him something.

"Oh by the way how is that girl…umm I believe her name is Beth!" I hissed walking pass him and downstairs to the kitchen.

"What…I don't know and personally I don't want to know anything about her!" he spat back at me following me into the kitchen.

"Oh by the way speaking of secrets we have kept from each other…what is with the kids… I mean I thought you didn't have any…and where may I asked is the Daddy!" he hissed at me.

"Oh and by the way…how is your family your sisters Ashley and Jackie?" he asked concerned.

When I heard Jackie's name I was instantly brought to tears as I turned on my heels and left the kitchen and went up to my room as I quickly closed the door behind me with a slam.

~*~

CHAPTER THIRTY

"You shouldn't have asked that!" Meghan told Damian as she entered the room slowly.

"What?" he asked with a confused look.

"What did I say?" he asked as Meghan left the room.

Damian looked towards the top of the stairs as he was so confused by my reactions. With some hesitation Damian started climbing the stairs.

I slid down the door and cried at the mention of my sister's name. I thought I was past all this pain from the loss of my sister. I was also upset by seeing Damian again and learning he was my next-door neighbor. I thought I was also over losing Damian too but I guess I'm not over it at all. All I wanted was to run into Damian's arms and have him hold me and never let go ever but he didn't want me anymore and the fact was that within a few months he would surely be with Beth forever.

"God Damian why show up again in my life...just when I thought I was over him and over the death of my sister...everything comes flooding back!"

I heard a knock at my door and I quickly wiped my tears from my face.

"Kayla...honey please let me in...I didn't mean to upset you!" he whispered.

"GO AWAY...GET THE FUCK OUT OF HERE!" I screamed as I hit the door with my fist.

"Kayla…please I'm sorry if I said something to upset you…ooooh dam it I don't like talking through a door…just let me in!" he hissed as he hit the door.

"I need to talk to you face to face…god I could use a friend too!" he said quietly.

Damian kept banging on the door and finally I broke even though I was still hurt and mad at him the truth was I could use at least a friend now as I started this new venture in my life. I truly had no clue of what to do next. I cautiously opened the door and walked over and plopped myself down on my bed. My eyes started watering once again as I felt Damian's touch on my leg.

"Kayla…baby please talk to me I'm sorry if I said something to upset you!" he said while touching my leg.

"I can't talk to you!" I said as my tears fell.

"Why baby please obviously…you are in so much pain…talking might just help a wee bit…look I have these two big broad shoulders…as a matter of fact I hear that they are just perfect to cry on …and I also have been told I'm a good listener!" he said we a heartwarming smile.

I looked at him and tried to smile…but by this point I found it harder to smile anymore and my world was consumed with darkness. I couldn't believe that I was still crying tears as over the last days and months I thought I was surely drained. Damian wiped the tears from my eyes and waited for me to speak.

~*~

CHAPTER THIRTY-ONE

"The thing is well my sister Ashley is fine…and as for Jackie!" my tears fell again.

"Yeah!" he said with concern.

"Oh god Jackie is gone…oh god how can I possibly be those babies' mom…yeah me Damian can you imagine me a mom…oh god I don't know the first thing about that!" I said as I began crying harder.

With what I just said and by the look upon Damian's face told me he was feeling like the biggest smuck in the world.

Damian stood by waiting for me to finish up before saying anything. I continued pacing back and forth.

"I can't believe Jackie wants me to raise her children!" I cried.

"Omg…Kayla I'm so sorry about your sister…I had no ideal!" he said as he pulled me into an embrace.

I just let myself fall into Damian's arms I was so mentally drained by the last few months. I had no clue how I had pulled the last couple months off.

"Kayla…Jackie obviously has a lot of faith in you…to raise her kids!"

"Do you really think so?" I asked as I pulled away from him to look in his beautiful blue eyes.

"I really do Kayla… you turned your business into the top talent management company in the world… that takes guts and extremely hard work and huge responsibility…you did that on your own… you will do just fine…believe in yourself!" he said as he looked back at me wiping my tears.

"I have…haven't I…but I do have amazing people that work for me!" I replied and grin a little.

I caught his gaze and we stood there just looking in each other's eyes. I wanted so much for Damian to tell me he wants me but soon I remembered what he had said to me a few months earlier. I pulled from his embrace and walked out of the room and back down the stairs to finish unloading the truck.

"Dam it Kayla…I need you so badly!" he whispered with frustration and soon joined me at the truck.

As he walked to the back of the truck I couldn't help but keep him in my sight. I placed a couple of boxes in front of him and he graciously took them. I grabbed a couple more boxes and took them into the kitchen and started putting them away. I watched Damian from the kitchen as he interacted with my nieces and nephew. They seem to like him very much. As the day progress Damian was helping us so much. Damian had taken a seat at the counter in front of me to rest.

"Aunt Mac…I'm hungry!" Meghan said as she looked up at me.

"Okay honey…give me a few minutes love!" I said as I picked her up.

"Alright…I love you!" Meghan said as she hugged me.

"I love you to…honey…go play in your room…I will call you when I'm done!" I said as I returned her to the ground.

"Can I help you with dinner?" he asked as he walked around into the kitchen.

"If you want to…are you hungry Damian?" I asked with a smile.

"Yeah I'm famish!" he said as he patted his belly.

I walked over to the fridge and grabbed out some hamburger meat to make hamburgers.

"Damian can you grab some side dishes from the pantry…please!" I asked with a smile.

"Sure no problem…is your grill here?" he asked.

"Yeah out under the gazebo thingy…I mean it's built right in!" I said as I took notice of Damian's bum and body as he walked into the pantry.

"You are so checking me out!" he said with a cheeky smile.

"I was not!" I said with embarrassment.

"Yes you are don't lie!" he said with a cheeky grin.

"Fine if you must know yes…but you just can't walk around looking so gorgeous…gosh I'm only human!" I said as I started making patties.

He smiled and places the side dishes on the island in the middle of my kitchen. He walked over to where I was and started making patties.

"Do you have a grill lighter?" he asked.

"Yeah in the drawer next to the dishwasher!" I replied.

Damian finished up making the patties and went outside as I put the patties on a serving dish and carried them out to him.

"You know you have a nice place here!" he said with a smile.

"Thank you…when I saw this house I knew this place was the one!" I said as I stood with my back against the wall looking at him.

"Yes I so know what you mean!" he said as he placed the hamburgers on the grill.

I sat down on the wall as Damian made his way over to me. He started rubbing my legs as he looked at me.

"Kayla…do you think about us?" he asked still rubbing my thighs.

"What about it?" I asked trying hard not to be overly excited.

"Kayla…about us finding a way back to each other!" he said with tears welling up in his eyes.

"I really should go fix the rest of dinner!" I said as I hopped down from the wall. I couldn't talk about us because I still wanted an us so badly but I was so scared.

"Kayla…answer me!" he said as he tried following me.

"Dam it…Kayla I want you back!" he said softly as he tended to the grill.

I could feel my tears starting to fall because I wanted him so much.

As I tended to the other stuff all I could think of was Damian and I. I grabbed the plates from the cupboard and I sat the table so we could eat as soon as Damian was done. Damian made his way in and placed the hamburgers on the table and everyone started digging in. I watched Damian from across the table as he did me.

After dinner I told the kids to bathe and get ready for bed as we were going to watch a movie. Damian helped me with the kitchen and then we headed into the family room to watch a movie. The kids each grabbed their pillows and blankets and lay on the floor as Damian and I sat on the couch.

~*~

CHAPTER THIRTY-TWO

Halfway through the movie the kids fell asleep. I woke the older ones to go on up to bed. As Damian carried Meghan up the stairs as I showed Damian the way to Meghan's room.

"Goodnight Aunt Mac...I love you!" she replied sleepily.

"Goodnight my dear...I love you so much!" I whispered back as I tucked her in the blankets.

"Goodnight Damian...see you!" she replied sleepily.

"Goodnight honey!" he replied and stepped out into the hall.

"Aunt Mac...Damian is so nice...and I think he likes you a lot Aunt Mac!" she whispered.

"Ya Damian is sweet...now go to sleep you!" I said as I turned on her nightlight and turned off the light.

I walked back out to the hall and closed the door slightly.

"I guess you have another fan!" I said as I leaned against the wall.

"Yeah your nieces and nephew are something else...I like them too!" he replied as he moved in closer to me.

"Kayla...I miss you!" he said, as he was now only inches from my lips.

I looked at him and once again I got lost in his eyes.

"I...I miss you too!" I whispered as I moved closer.

Before we knew it Damian started attacking my lips with his.

"Thank you for today…and dinner…I need to get back home!" he said as he pulled away from me and turned and started walking downstairs.

I followed closely behind him and he opened the door and turned and smiled at me and winked and walked outside. As he got to the end of the yard where his yard meets mine he turned and waved.

"Bye Kayla…see you in the morning!" he said and disappeared onto his front porch.

I waved back at him and went back inside and up to my room. I flicked on the light and started undressing as Damian watched from his bedroom window.

I stopped as I realized my windows were opened. I got over to the window and gazed out to see familiar eyes looking at me. Damian just smiled with his bare chest exposed. He waved as he continued messing with his pants. I couldn't help but sneak one last peak at this manly specimen. My body was still reeling from his tender kiss he had planted upon my lips. It took everything in me not to pounce on him and drag him into my room and have my way with him.

I smiled and closed the blinds in my room.

"Oh god his room faces mine, this could be quite interesting and fun" I said with a smirk.

I finished undressing and headed in to take my bath. I started running my bath water and added bubble bath. I slipped into the huge roman tub and slowly sat down and let the warm bubble engulf my body. All I could think of was Damian I missed him so much.

"Stop this girl you are just going through a tuff time right now…you are so vulnerable right now…and besides Beth had Damian all to herself now!"

All I could do right now is just cry for my dead sister and cry and think about what could be or come about between Damian and I.

~*~

CHAPTER THIRTY-THREE

I rolled over to look at the clock and it was about 9am. I could hear the kids were up and already started to fight with each other. I flung the covers off of me and headed downstairs to see what the problem was.

"What the heck is the problem here?" I asked as I walked into the kitchen.

"Aunt Mac …Ben won't put his turtle back in its cage!" Jenna said at the top of her voice.

"Oh my god!" I said as I tried to pick up the turtle off the table.

About this time Damian had made his way through the back door right in the midst of the madness.

"Good morning everybody!" he said as he sat a bag of groceries down on the counter.

I looked over at Damian about ready to pull my hair out in the midst of the chaos.

"Honey take a seat while I make everyone some breakfast!" he said whilst handing me a Starbuck vanilla latté.

I must have looked at him with confusion in my eyes. That he took my hand and walked me over towards the counter where I sat down.

"Is your latte` okay or do you need some more sugar?" he asked me with a smile.

I took a small sip of my latte` and shook my head no.

"Okay now you all need to quiet down and find something to do while I make some breakfast…where does this thing go?" he asked as he looked at me as he picked up the turtle.

"Umm…on the back porch in the fish tank…I will show you!" I said as I got off the stool and led him out the French doors.

Damian followed me out the door and he gently put the turtle he was holding into the tank. After he put the turtle back he looked over at me as he placed a hand on my shoulder.

"How are you holding up Kayla?" he asked as he turned me to face him.

"How am I doing…I just don't know anymore…they are driving me crazy…I swear I'm failing miserably!" I said on the brink of tears.

"Hey now don't say that…I think you are doing the best you can under the circumstances…you know what I think?" he asked me as he lifted my chin to look at him.

"What Damian…what do you think!" I asked him as I looked deeply in his eyes.

"I think you all could use a day of fun…after breakfast everyone will get dressed and we can all just have a day of fun…okay babe!" he said as he pulled me into a hug.

"Come on what do you say?" he said as he touched my face.

"Damian honey I really don't know!" I said with hesitation.

"Please Kayla…it will be fun!" he said as he held me.

"Alright…fun sounds good!" I said with a smile.

~*~

CHAPTER THIRTY-FOUR

After breakfast I told the kids to go upstairs and get ready for an outing. I helped Meghan get dressed and went into my room to shower and dressed. I walked into my closet to figure out what to wear. I settled on a pair of hip hugger jeans with a button down shirt that only buttoned half way and bared my mid-drift with a pair of mesh tennis shoes. I put my hair up with a clip and let some loose hair fall along either side of my face.

I grabbed my purse and cell phone and headed downstairs. As I walked downstairs I saw Damian looking up at me and I flashed him a smile and made my descent down the stairs. Damian met me at the bottom of my stairs and brushed my hair from my face.

"Umm…is there ever a day that you don't look good?" he asked me as he put on his sunglasses.

"Umm…I don't recall!" I said with a chuckle as Damian grabbed my hand and walked me out the door as the kids followed.

I quickly closed and locked my front door after turning on my alarm. Damian led me to his Mercedes SUV and opened my door for me as the kids crawled into the backseat. Damian shut my door and walked around and got into the driver's seat. He looked in his rear view mirror.

"Okay…buckle up…and here we go!" he said as he started backing out the driveway.

Damian immediately started fiddling with the radio as he drove on.

The song Can't Get You Out of My Head came on the radio and he started singing along with the radio. He sang horribly off key and the kids and I Started laughing.

"Okay so what is so funny huh!" he said grin.

"You are singing way off key…and to think you get paid to do this professionally!" I said in a matter of a fact kind of way.

"Yeah…I do don't I!" he giggled.

The kids looked on at us and then Meghan began to speak.

"What does that mean…Aunt Mac?" she asked.

"Umm…that mean Damian was in a very successful band called Savage Garden…but now Damian is now a solo artist…he has songs on the radio!" I went on.

"Umm…that is actually how I met Damian…I was going to be his manager!" I went on as I started remembering how we started out.

"OMG…really you sing on the radio?" all the kids started chiming in.

"So umm…do you know singers?" Jenna started inquiring.

"Yeah I know some singers…there are some I still would like to meet myself!" he went on.

"Do you know Madonna?" Jenna asked again as she started moving forward.

"Umm…yeah I know her…she an interesting person and an awesome artist.

All the kids seemed more intrigued with Damian the more they found out about him.

"Aunt Mac why does Damian talk funny?" Meghan asked me.

"That is because he wasn't born in America…he was born in Australia!" I went on as I looked over at Damian.

"Oh…I remember when you went there and when you came home…Mommy and you were talking…you said Australian men are awesome lovers and they rocked you all night long!" Meghan blurted out.

"Meghan…shhh!" Jenna interrupted.

"Jenna that is okay…please go on Meghan…this is quite an intriguing topic we are talking about!" Damian said as he started chuckling.

"Kids you know they say the darnest things!" I said to Damian as I slid down in my seat further. Just then Damian pulled up a mall. I thought to myself thank god saved by the mall. Damian pulled up in a parking space and turned off the car. The kids all started piling out of the car leaving Damian and I alone. He looked over at me with a smirk.

"Umm…don't think we won't bring this up at a later date!" he started giggling as he opened his door and stepped out. He came around to my side and opened my door. He helped me out and we all started walking towards the entrance.

~*~

CHAPTER THIRTY-FIVE

Damian reached over and grabbed my hand as we started walking around the mall. Ben saw the arcade and wanted to go in.

"First…we need to buy school clothes…and then we can do that next!" I said as we headed for Old Navy. We went in and Jenna went to her section and then Ben went over to his section with Damian. I took Meghan to her next to Jenna's section. I let Jenna look around and start picking out stuff as I started looking around with Meghan.

We picked out a couple of skirts and pants and shirts. As she showed me I looked over at Damian who seems to be handling Ben okay.

Damian met my gaze and he started smiling at me I smiled back.

He held up a couple of things Ben had picked out and I shook my head yes. I stood there watching him as Jenna and Meghan saw the way we were looking at each other.

"Jenna…I think Aunt Mac likes Damian…and I think he likes her back!" she went on.

"Yeah…I think you are right…you know I think they were a couple once!" she said as she pulled a shirt off the rack for Meghan.

"You think so…I wonder what made Aunt Mac so mad at him!" she went on.

"Look Meghan…sometimes things don't work out…who knows they might get back together again…she seems so happy when he is around!" Jenna went on still looking at the clothes.

"So how you two coming along?" I asked them as I turned around to talk to the girls.

"Yeah…I think I'm done!" they both said in unison.

"Okay…let's go check on Ben and Damian shall we?" I said to them.

We grabbed the things and we walked over to Ben and Damian. Damian helped Ben pick out some stuff but he wanted to check with me first.

I went through the clothes and we made our way over to the check-out counter.

As the girl checked us out Damian started working his fingers into mine. The girl told me the total and I reached into my purse for my wallet when Damian gave a credit card to the girl.

"Damian I got this…you don't have to!" I started to say as he placed a finger over my lips to quiet me.

"I insist Kayla…it will be my pleasure!" he said as he signed the slip.

We left the store and went into a few others where I got the kids more things and then we went into a shoe store. Every store Damian paid for everything it kind of made me mad.

But as he explained about how he spoils his sister and brother's kids. I kind of understood where he was coming from and how much he seems to love kids.

"Are you all hungry?" he asked us.

We all shook our heads and headed for The Rainforest Café for lunch. Damian left the table to use the restroom as Ben followed leaving the girls with me.

"Aunt Mac…Damian seems to be a nice guy!" Jenna went on.

"Yeah he sure is…I love him!" I said not realizing what I just said.

"So you and Damian were a couple once?" Jenna said waiting for an answer.

"Yeah…we were!" was all I said as I thought back to happier times.

"What happened?" Jenna went on.

"Umm…long story!" I said still thinking about the times.

Just then Damian and Ben came back to the table and Damian took a seat next to me. The kids looked over the menu as did Damian and I.

We gave the server our order and waited for our drinks.

"So Damian…how is it like in Australia?" Ben started asking him.

"Umm…it is different…my family lives there…my family will be coming for a visit in a few weeks…so you all will meet them!" Damian went on.

"Really…I bet you can't wait huh!" I said to him.

"Yeah it has been a while since I saw them…my parents we be celebrating their 30th wedding anniversary…I would like it very much Kayla if you would help me plan it…I have a few appointments about it tomorrow…will you come with me?" he asked.

"Umm…I really can't leave the kids by themselves!" I informed him.

"Layne is taking Calvin to the zoo…she would take the kids!" he said.

"Umm…I will think about it okay!' I said with a smile.

We talked all through lunch and then went to the arcade and then to a movie and headed home afterwards.

The kids fell asleep in the car on the way back home. Along the way Damian held my hand as we talked. Damian pulled up at my house and parked his suv. He helped me carry Meghan in the house as Ben and Jenna barely followed us in. I told the kids to thank Damian for the day and for lunch and dinner and the clothes and shoes. They did and the older ones' bathe and went to bed. After getting the kids settled in he got back on the topic of the party and I told him I would help him. Later on Damian called Lea and she agreed to take the kids to the zoo. It turned out that Lea was interested in Jenna for babysitting maybe a couple hours so Robert and her could have some grown up time. I also told Damian that I wouldn't mind watching Calvin for her either.

Where did I go anymore now having the kids? But I really didn't mind much. That night Damian and I watched a couple movies and talked about the party for his parents. We said our goodnights and I headed on up to shower and bed. I started undressing in front of my window and Damian watched me. We stood there looking at each other for the longest time.

~*~

CHAPTER THIRTY- SIX

About 10 am the next morning there was a knock at my front door. I got up to answer the door. I opened the front door and saw Damian and Lea standing there.

Good morning baby!" he exclaimed as he pulled me in for an embrace.

"Morning…hello Lea it is great to see you again!" I said with a smile.

"Hello Makayla…it is great to see you too!" she said as smile crept across her face.

"Thank you so much for taking the kids today…I really appreciate it!" I said as I extended my hand to shake hers.

"Hey now we are huggers here…and no problem it just beats me having to plan the party!" she said with a laugh.

"Okay now I suddenly feel liked I am going to regret this!" I said as I looked over at Damian.

"No you won't it just me I hate doing that kind of stuff!" Lea reassured me.

"Okay…kids Lea is here…she ready to leave!" I called out to the kids.

They all came running over to the front door to meet her.

"Okay this is Jenna, Ben and Meghan…you all better make sure you mind Lea…or you all will be in big trouble!" I said aloud as I kissed them.

"We will, bye Aunt Mac…love you!" they all said in unison.

"Have fun loves…be good…thanks Lea I owe you!" I said with that they were out the door.

Layne's husband Robert was waiting in the car for the kids. Damian and I stood in the doorway watching them leave.

As they pulled away Damian turned to look at me.

"Well I guess we are on our own!" he said with a smirk.

"Yeah I guess so…are you ready to leave?" I asked with a smile.

"Ready when you are…my car or yours?" he asked me.

"It doesn't matter to me!" I was quick to say.

"I just need to go get my purse and keys!" I let him know.

"Okay…hurry back love!" he said as he grabbed my hand.

I just stood there looking in his beautiful blue eyes. As we stood there Damian and I just gazed in each other's eyes as he pulled me into an embrace.

He pulled me into to a passionate kiss. I couldn't control myself any longer and I fell into his arms. His kiss felt like fire upon my skin burning my flesh.

"Oh god…we aren't going to get anywhere doing this!" I whispered breathlessly.

"You are right!" he said as he picked me up and carried me up to my room.

We kissed along the way as if nothing has ever come between us. I longed to be in his arms but I couldn't stop thinking about Beth.

He laid me upon my bed as he started unbuttoning my shirt.

"We can't do this baby…god how I love you!" I said with tears.

I pulled away from him as I held my hand to my mouth as if I just let slip my greatest secret.

"If you love me and I love you what is the problem!" he said quietly.

"God Damian you do love me!" I said with shock.

Tears started rolling down my cheeks as he admitted his most inner secret out. He pulled away and started pacing about my room running his fingers through his dark hair.

~*~

CHAPTER THIRTY-SEVEN

I looked at Damian and he looked at me and neither one knew what to say next. We stood there waiting and wanting so much for one to start speaking. Still nothing until I thoughtfully thought about what to say next.

"We should get going what you say?" he spoke up.

I couldn't believe what he just said to me all I could do was just agree with him but I knew this wouldn't be the last we spoke about this.

All I had to know is that he still loves me after all this time and now I knew I could be stronger than I was before. I had his love and he belongs to me.

I just followed behind him still thinking about what he had just admitted. Even though we've been apart these last few months doesn't mean I haven't been thinking a great deal about him. I knew now that it could very well work between us even though Beth was in the picture. I could never keep him from his child if in fact it was his. I grabbed my purse and keys.

"Okay ready!" I said as I buttoned my shirt back up.

"Great umm…let's go!" he said quietly.

I followed Damian down the stairs and out through the garage after setting my alarm. I hit my key chain to unlock my car.

"I thought you would've got rid of this AMG by now!" he said making small talk.

"No…I just bought a SUV…when the kids and I go anywhere!" I said as I got into the driver's seat.

"Oh I see…not like I would get rid of it either…if I had this car!" he said as I just looked over at him.

"Where to first?" I asked as I backed out my driveway.

I came to a stop at the end of my driveway.

"I think maybe you should drive!" I said as I put my car in park.

"Really are you sure?" he asked me with hesitation.

"Yeah I really think so!" I said as I leaned back in my seat.

"Cool…I really think your car is awesome!" he said with a smile.

I got out of the car and walked over to the passenger side as Damian did the same. Damian sat down in the driver's seat with a huge smile on his face as if he got everything he wanted for Christmas.

"Can we put the top down?" he asked.

"I don't see why not!" I said with a grin as I hit the switch.

Damian got settled and started to leave the drive and ease his way into the traffic on the street.

Shortly after we pulled into a caterer shop that was also in the same building as the party planner. The receptionist asked the name and told us to take a seat and that they would be right with us. After a few minutes a man came over to us and introduced himself.

"Hello I'm Jim…so what can I help you with…wait don't answer let me guess a wedding right…you will be such a gorgeous bride and a very handsome groom…if I do say so!" he said as he kissed my cheek and shake Damian's hand.

"Oh umm…no we aren't getting married!" he said with a slight giggle in his voice.

"Oh I'm so sorry…I guess I just assumed…you all make such a gorgeous couple!" Jim was quick to correct himself.

"No harm done…it really is an anniversary party for my Mum and Dad…in a few weeks when they come for a visit!" Damian said with a smile.

"Oh…I see…how many years may I ask?" Jim replied.

"It will be their 30th!" Damian said with a smile.

"Wow that is a long time…relax Mr. Starr leave it to me…I will make it beautiful!" he said as we all took a seat at his desk.

"Good I'm counting on you!" he said with a grin.

We started looking over different themes for the party, then Damian turned to look at me.

"Makayla…help me out…what do you think love?" he asked as he placed his hand on mine.

"Umm…Damian I think maybe a luau might be cute if you are planning it by your pool!" I suggested to him.

"You know I think you are on to something there!" he said as he rubbed the top of my hand.

"You know Makayla is right that could be awesome for a pool party!" Jim said with a smile on his face.

~*~

CHAPTER THIRTY-EIGHT

Damian and I were still looking over different things while back at Damian's place Beth had showed up. Beth checked each door on the property until she found a door to enter through that happened to be a door off the garage. Beth let herself in and noticed Damian's car was still in the garage. She got excited thinking that Damian was still home.

As she drove up she noticed the house next door had finally got sold and people had moved in.

"I hope that it is a married woman not a single!" she thought to herself as she was starting to feel threaten.

So Beth crept into the kitchen and started looking around and then made a walk through the house and realized Damian wasn't home.

"Okay I guess I will just have to wait!" she said aloud.

Beth grabbed something to eat and went into the living room to watch some TV. Back at the party planners Damian and I were sampling some of the great dishes Jim had prepared. Damian and I were having an awesome time. We finally picked the entrees and the theme and Damian started writing out a check to leave a deposit for Jim.

We finally were done and we were getting ready to leave when Jim told Damian to remember him just in case we decided to plan a wedding any time soon. Damian and I walked back to the car and Damian opened my car door.

"Are you hungry Kayla?" he asked me.

"Well you know I could eat…all that food was just a tease!" I told him with a smile.

Damian noticed I had some cake on my face when he reaches over with hanky and wiped my face tenderly.

After that Damian lean in and placed a tender kiss on my lips.

"What was that for?" I asked him as he stood back a bit to look at me.

"Thank you so much for helping me today!" he said softly.

"Your welcome I was glad to help!" I said as I turned to get in the car.

Damian pulled me into an embrace and started kissing me passionately. I once again fell into his kiss as I wrapped my arms about him. We stood there for a while just kissing each other.

"We should get going!" he said as he broke the embrace.

He walked around the car and got in the driver seat as I pulled my door shut. I was so puzzled by Damian actions towards me. It made me upset because I can't switch gears that fast like him. I was growing

weaker by the moments each time he touched me.

Beth was growing more impatient by the minutes she decided she wanted to take a nap. She decided she would nap in his bed upstairs.

Damian and I went to lunch and drank a whole bottle of wine as we talked all through and soon we lost track of time. We were having such a great time that he thought we should go looking through old antiques shops. By the time we were heading back it was night. We pulled into my garage Damian put the car in park and once again we were gazing at each other. He pulled me into an embrace and started kissing me. This time was different he seems to be not holding back. He almost smothered me by his kisses as he pulled back and this time he pulled the keys out of the ignition and got out of the car.

He walked over to my side and opened my door and yanked me out of my seat and pulled me behind him. He unlocked my door and I turned off my alarm as once again he attacked my lips and I attacked his during the process we knocked things of the walls as we flung each other against the other wall. Damian started grabbing at my clothes and me at his.

"God Love…you are so dam sexy!" he whispered in between kisses.

"You are so gorgeous!" I whispered back at him.

"I need you so badly Kayla!" he moaned.

He pulled my shirt apart and pulled it off me exposing my bra. He then pulled off my bra as he started suckling on my breast. I started feeling butterflies in my stomach as he touched me. I ripped his shirt off his back as I started kissing his nipples and chest.

I started unbuttoning his button fly jeans as I pulled at his belt. I freed his jeans off his hips as I went to my knees freeing his manhood from his boxers. I grabbed his shaft as I started licking and sucking his manhood.

"Oh god yes…mmm Kayla!" he moaned.

The more I pleasured him he seems to moan louder and louder.

"Oh god yes...yes!" he moaned as he came into my mouth.

He collapsed against the wall as he got his breathing back. He pulled his pants back up and fastened them halfway. He pulled me up to meet his lips as he pressed them to mine. He then lifted me into his arms and started carrying me up the stairs to my room.

Along the way we were kissing passionately. He struggled with my door until I helped him out as he closed the door with his foot. He put me on my feet as he once again attacked my lips. He pulled the rest of my clothing off my body and we started kissing again while he backing me up to my bed.

Beth woke up and noticed it was dark now and Damian was nowhere in sight. Just to make sure he wasn't home she walked over to his window and looked out. She noticed a light on across the way and wanted to check the person out.

Beth saw the window blinds were opened and noticed two figures in the window across the way. Beth rubbed her eyes when she noticed Damian in the window.

"What Damian...omg!" was all she could say.

"It can't be!" she whispered.

"What the hell is he doing there?" she started questioning.

The more she watched she knew that the two figures were kissing each other. As she watched she begins to realize

Damian and the lady was in the midst of a heated moment. Beth became angrier by the minute and she knew there was only one thing to do.

~*~

CHAPTER THIRTY-NINE

"I love you Kayla...I never have stopped loving you!" he whispered.

"I love you Damian...make love to me please!" I begged him.

With that Damian and I fell to the bed as we started kissing passionately.

I once again pulled at Damian's pants as he tried to help the best he could. Both of us laid there naked as we started caressing each other's bodies.

"I need you baby!" I whispered breathlessly.

"Are you sure my love?" he asked tenderly.

"I want this more than ever...make love to me!" I whispered to him.

With that he started kissing me as the both of us started roaming each other's body.

"Oh god I love you!" I whispered in his ear.

"I love you too baby...I have wanted so long to hold you again!" he whispered as he ran his fingers through my long blonde hair.

His words were so sweet and sincere he melted my heart with his words. I felt as if we were the only two people in the world and I knew then that Damian and I had a bond that could never be broken again.

All I knew in that moment is that I loved him more than ever. He rolled me onto my belly as he started kissing my back tenderly. His lips on my skin sent chills throughout my body. I then rolled back on my back as I wrapped my arms about his neck. As he started leaving trails of baby kisses down my torso.

We once again fell together as one and let our inhibitions take over. We fell into each other as we start pleasuring each other's.

After Beth saw what was going on she decided she would leave a few things around Damian house so there was no way someone wouldn't miss things. She was slowly coming undone she knew she just had to bring Damian back to her. Beth was fuming as she left Damian's place she felt as if he was slipping away from her. Damian and I drifted off to sleep. As we slept Damian sleep was soon interrupted as he started remembering little tidbits of information about the night he was with Beth. Damian rolled over and held me up against him hoping he could force Beth out of mind. I let out a slight moan as I wrapped my arms about his body. That night we slept with such an inner peace deep inside of us.

~*~

CHAPTER FORTY

The next morning Damian lay awake looking over at me.

"Oh god why do I always feel so tired the next morning after a night of sex!" he thought to himself.

He lay there looking at me as the sun crept through the open blinds. He loved the way my hair glisten in the sun and the way it lit my face.

"God how I love you Kayla...I have missed you so much...I truly feel we can make it!" he said softly as he traced my face.

I started stirring as Damian lay awake watching.

"Good morning my love!" he said as he placed a gentle kiss on my lips.

"Good morning...baby how you sleep!" I asked him.

"I slept okay...better than I have in months!" he whispered as he kisses my torso.

"Are you hungry my love?" I asked as I started to get up.

"Hey where you going?" he asked me as he pulled me down on top of him.

We started kissing passionately as he pulled my robe off my shoulders.

He laid me back against my bed as he moved on top of me. He slowly ran his hands down my arms tenderly. He started leaving a trail of baby kisses down my torso. We once again fell as one and started making love slowly and tenderly. Soon after we brought each other to orgasmic bliss. We both lay back against my bed and felt our heartbeats coming down.

"So are you hungry yet?" he asked me.

"Yeah I could go for some…you want me to fix us something?" I asked as I kissed Damian's lips.

"How about we both cook?" he suggested as he returned my kiss.

We both started getting up as I put his shirt on and he pulled on his pants. I started making my way downstairs as Damian followed behind grabbing at my body. We both giggled as we made our way down to the kitchen.

"Where do we start?" he said with a laughed.

I grabbed the pancake mix from the pantry and Damian started looking through the cabinets for a bowl. I grabbed a pan and some water and oil to make the pancakes. Damian started setting the table and put juice in our glasses. He came up behind me and helped me stir the batter as he placed a soft kiss upon my neck. We sat down at the table and started talking and eating our breakfast. Damian reached across the table and grabbed my hand. I let out a slight sigh as his touches made me weak.

"Do you have some coffee?" he asked me softly.

"Yes…let me get some started for you okay!" I said as I got up from the table.

As I walked over to the counter I turned to face Damian again as I flashed him a smile. He looked over at me and smiled tenderly at me.

In that moment we connected once more I felt so happy having Damian to wake up with. This morning I didn't feel as lonely as I have in the past months. I poured Damian a cup of coffee and brought it over to the table and sat it in front of him.

"Well I guess we better get dressed before the kids get here!" he said as he sipped his coffee.

"Yeah I guess you are right!" I said as I put the dishes in the sink.

Damian and I made our way up to my room and into the bathroom.

We both got in the shower as Damian started looking me up and down.

"What are you looking at?" I asked him after letting the water cascade along my body.

"I'm looking at you my love, the way the water seems to hug your figure, the sun the way it lights your face!" he whispered softly.

With that Damian found my lips as he slowly and tenderly tasted the sweetness of my lips. His tongue eagerly found mine as I slowly began running my fingers along his skin leaving goose bumps up and down much as I loved his kisses we both knew we needed to stop as the kids would soon be coming home from spending the night with Layne and Robert's.

~*~

CHAPTER FORTY-ONE

"Well I guess we should stop before…we get going again!" he said with a giggle.

"Yeah I guess you got a point there!" I said with a giggle as I rinsed my hair out.

Damian held my body in his arms as I rinsed my hair. Damian ran a finger along my torso and brushed his finger along my red lips.

"God you are so beautiful Kayla!" as he raised me up as he attacked my lips once more.

"I love you so much!" I whispered in between kisses.

"I love you too my love!" he whispered back at me.

After a few minutes Damian and I got out of the shower and dried off.

"I need to go and get some of my clothes at my house…would you like to walk with, we still have about an hour before Lea brings the kids back?" Damian said in a matter of fact way.

"Okay just let me get dressed!" I said softly.

Damian dressed in what he was wearing the day before as I walked into my closet. I picked a white terry tank shirt and a drawstring terry mini. I put on my scandals and took a look in my mirror. I put my long blonde curly hair up in a clip.

"Okay ready when you are!" I said as I blew him a kiss.

Damian smiled and came up behind me and wrapped his arms around my waist as I smiled at him in the mirror.

"I'm glad we have another chance at love again!" he said with a smile and a soft kiss on my neck.

"Me too baby…you can't know how miserable I was without you in my life these last few months!" I said with tears building in my eyes.

"Oh honey don't cry I'm here for you now…no one will ever come between us ever again!" he said with a smile as he wiped my tears that had escaped.

With that Damian and I walked down stairs and out the front door and across our yards. We got to his front door and Damian grabbed his keys from his pocket.

I waited as he opened his door as I leaned against the wall. He finally opened the door and he reached for my hand and pulled me inside his place. As I looked around I couldn't help but see how beautifully elegant his house was done up. I followed him up the stairs and into a huge master bedroom with an awesome view of the bay.

"Your house is beautiful!" I said with a smile.

"Thank you honey!" he said with a smile as he walked into his bathroom.

As he walked into his bathroom I looked around his room and finally taking a seat on his bed. I lay down upon his bed as I sprawled out across his bed. As I lay down I took in his scent that was on his bed.

How I loved the scent of him the touch of his skin the way I feel when I'm in his arms. I put my arms around his pillow as I put my arm under the pillow I pulled out a red bra.

~*~

CHAPTER FORTY-TWO

I quickly got up from the bed and my thoughts were so scattered.

"Was Damian still with her…or was it her way to try and control the situation!" I was lost in my thoughts when Damian made his way out of the bathroom.

Damian saw the red bra thrown on the ground as he looked over at me.

"Kayla I swear I don't know where this came from!" he said with a scared look on his face.

"Damian I know!" I said as I moved closer to him.

Damian quickly grabbed some things and we left and we went back to my house. We both went into the living room and sat down on the sofa. I noticed something different in his eyes since we left his house.

"Damian are you okay honey… Is something is bothering…please talk to me!" I said as I knelt down in front of him.

Damian looked down at me and touched my cheek tenderly.

Damian had a looked on his face I could tell something was wrong with him.

"Promise me I can tell you anything and you won't be mad at me!" he said with a serious look on his face.

"Sure baby…I promise not to get mad at you…please Damian just tell me what you have to say!" I said a little worried and apprehension.

I wasn't quite sure if I was truly ready to hear what his confession.

"God where do I begin!" he started to say.

I sat there on the threshold of doubt just waiting for him to tell me what was on his mind.

"It's about Beth honey…it just umm…I sometimes doubt that night we were together!" he started to say very nervously.

"What about it!" I said with a hint of a tear clinging to my voice.

"It's umm…I really don't think I slept with her!" he went on.

"I don't understand honey…what do you mean by that!" I said with hesitation.

"I've been having dreams lately about that night!" he went on.

I sat there listening intently as I waited for him to continue.

~*~

CHAPTER FORTY-THREE

"Like what kind of dreams have you been having?" I asked wanting to get to the truth.

"Well it's more like day dreams really…and fact I know about myself…like when we have had sex the next morning I wake up more tired kind of drained!" he said as he started pacing the room.

"I had one dream where I come to…and I remember her hitting me for some reason!" he went on.

"Why would she do that for?" I asked him as I went over to the window to look out.

"I really don't know…she seems very angry with me!" he went on.

"I remember drinking but I never drink enough to get fall down drunk!" he said as he moved closer to me.

"I remember she went into the bathroom…I took a seat in a chair…I remember her taking a while!" he went on.

I stood there looking out the window listening to all he was saying to me and it started my own wheels turning in my head.

"I next remember I asked her for a glass of water when she came out…she went into kitchen as I followed her but took a seat in the living room!" he said trying to work his way out the fog in his mind.

"So I drank the glass of water… I remember my head started hurting and she gave me an aspirin…she also told me I could lay down and I did…then everything got real foggy then…then I started to fall asleep…I swear Kayla I don't remember sleeping with her…then next is me waking up a little and feeling cold and her yelling something at me…she seemed very angry with me…then next thing I woke the next morning naked with her sleeping next to her and I quickly got up and dressed and left before she even woke!" he finished off.

"Kayla please say you believe me love…I have felt this way for a long time…everything about that night just don't make sense to me…I never wanted to say anything for fear of upsetting you…but I knew when she called I had no choice but to tell you about her!" he said as he pulling me into an embrace.

"Yes…honey I believe you I really do my love…and I swear we will get to the bottom of this together…I love you baby!" I said as I fell into his embrace.

Damian and I sat down on the couch as we both starting taking from the conversation what each wanted too. I knew something wasn't right about all he told me about. Our thoughts were interrupted with the ringing of the doorbell. I got up and walked over to the front door to answer it.

When I opened the door I was greeted by my nieces and nephews. They almost knocked me down as they all wrapped their arms about me.

"Hello there how was your trip to the zoo?" I asked as Damian helped me to my feet.

"Hello Layne thank you so much again with the kids!" I said as I hugged her.

"My pleasure dear...no worries... the kids were awesome!" she said as she kissed my cheek.

"Say can you take Calvin...I need to talked to Damian for a minute...do you mind dear?" she asked.

"Sure no problem...how about some coffee?" I asked her as I took Calvin in my arms and headed for the kitchen.

"So how was your time with Kayla?" Layne asked Damian as they walked out to the pool area.

"Omg...she still loves me...and we are going to try again!" he said with a cheeky grin.

"Really that is great Damian...you two belong together...not with that psycho Beth...she is bad news I don't trust her Damian!" she said as she hugged Damian.

"We stayed the night together Lea...I'm so happy I love her so much Lea!" he said as he backed away from Lea.

"I kind of figured that out Damian...that is why I took the kids for Kayla...so the two of you can work things out!" she said with a grin.

"You two make a cute couple...I think things will work out!" Lea said as she smiled at him.

"Thanks Lea...you are the best!" he said with a smile.

"Damian no thanks necessary…I know how miserable you were without her!" she smiled.

"How about that coffee now!" she said as they walked back into the house.

~*~

CHAPTER FORTY-FOUR

As the weeks past Damian and I were very discreet with the kids being around. The kids loved Damian more every single day. I got up and started cooking some breakfast for the kids when Damian was knocking at the back door. The kids rushed over to greet him at the door.

"Hello guys…how you are feeling this morning…I smelled a yummy breakfast cooking and thought I would join you!" he said as he winked at me.

"So Damian when are you going to stay overnight here?" Meghan started questioning him.

"Well umm…really not sure I guess Aunt Mac will have a say in that!" he said as he winked at me again.

"Guess what today is?" he asked the kids as the gathered at the table.

"Well umm…we all go to pick up my family at the airport later on today!" he said with excitement in his voice.

I was turned around at the stove when I started feeling sick at my tummy.

"Oh god!" I moaned as the smell of the bacon was getting to me.

"Kayla…honey what is wrong my love!" he said as he rushed over to my side.

"Nothing just smells getting to me…really haven't been feeling all that hot lately…no worries I'm okay!" I said as I walked over to the kitchen sink to splash water on my face.

"Why don't you take a shower nor have a seat and I will finish up for you…you know you are starting to look pea ken…are you sure you are alright love!" he asked me again.

"I already made an appointment with my doctors…but thank you I think I will sit for a few!" I said as I kissed him and took a seat at a high back chair sitting along the bar.

"Okay love…you want me to go with you to the doctors…when the appointment is!" he asked me.

"Oh it's on Monday along with the kids going back to school!" I said with a smile on my face.

"So when do we pick everyone up love?" I asked as he took over the job I had been doing.

"Oh it is about 3pm today!" he said with a wink.

Damian watched me closer that day for the rest of the day. We were all starting to dress for our outing when I went upstairs to get in the shower. I stepped into the shower and let the water cascade along my body. Damian followed me up to my room when he decided to slip into the shower with me.

"God I have been waiting all day to have some alone time with!" he said as he pulled me into a loving embrace.

"Oh you have huh!" I flirted with him as I placed a passionate kiss on his lips.

"Yeah I have!" he said with a chuckle as he attacked my lips once more.

"Well baby we have to wait a tad longer…we have to go get your family remember!" I whispered to him.

"Okay but promise me I can have you later on!" he started whimpering.

"Okay I promise honey!" I said to him with a smile.

Damian smiled and we both finished up our shower and we then dried off and dressed.

~*~

CHAPTER FORTY-FIVE

I walked into my walk-in closet and slipped on my silky mini skirt with a chiffon wrap blouse and some strappy sandals.

"Wow you look amazingly radiant!" Damian said as he walked out of the bathroom after doing his hair.

"Thank baby!" I said as I walked up to Damian and stole a kiss from him.

"Well what that is for…I so want you so badly!" he whispered in my ear as he started pawing on me.

"Well my dear you will have to wait until later!" I said with a flirty smile.

"Oh dam do I really have to wait…umm we could manage a little bit of time to you know!" he said as he gave me a playful childlike smile.

"Damian please we got to go get your parents!" I said to him as I started down the stairs.

"Kids…come on we got to get going!" I yelled out loud.

We all started heading out into the garage to take my Pearly White Cadillac Escalade. I hit the keychain to let everyone in as I threw the keys to Damian. Damian gave me a huge grin and got into the driver's side as I climbed into the passenger side. Damian backed out of the driveway and made his way into the street. On our way to the airport the kids were watching a movie as Damian watched the road as I watched out the window as Damian reached for my hand.

I looked over at Damian when I started feeling sick to my stomach.

"Honey…are you okay…the color just seems to drain from your face!" he said as he gave my hand a gentle squeeze.

"I'm okay baby really!" I said with a smile.

Shortly after we had arrived at the airport as we waited at the gate to greet his family. As we stood there I could see the look of anticipation on Damian's face, as it had been a long time since Damian had seen his family.

~*~

CHAPTER FORTY-SIX

"So are you excited to see your family?" I asked as I grabbed Damian's hand.

"Yeah it has been a while!" he said with a grin.

Just then there was an all call announcing the arrival of Damian's family's flight. Like clockwork the expression on his face changed from begin happy to begin totally ecstatic.

"Yeah I'm so excited...it has been a while since I've seen my family...like about a year...I haven't saw them since last Christmas!" Damian said with a look of excitement.

Just then a group of people started walking towards Damian and I and the kids.

"Mum...Dad!" Damian said with a smile as he hugged the both of them.

Damian broke his embrace as his Mum came in with a full fledge bear hug.

"Damian my handsome son...how are you doing...my love!" she said as she embraced him in a bear hug.

"I'm doing good...and you?" he asked with happy tears in his eyes as he dropped the embrace between his Mum and him.

"Dad...how are you doing man?" Damian asked as he shook his Dad's hand and then pulled him into an embrace.

"Great son...how are you buddy?" his Dad said while they were embracing.

"So little brother…how are you doing?" his sister Trish said as she ruffled her brother's hair.

"Trish…I'm good and you?" Damian asked as he pulled his sister into a bear hug.

"Doing just fine…sorry my brother is so inconsiderate…the name is Trish and this is my husband Paul and our kids Sarah and Benny!" Trish said as she extended her hand outward to shake my hand.

"It's a pleasure to meet you all!" I said as I stood beside Damian.

"Sorry family this is my beautiful girlfriend Makayla Weiss and these are her nieces Jena and Meghan and her nephew Ben as well!" Damian said standing there so proudly holding my hand.

"This is my brother Peter and his wife Tracy and their kids Peter, Sandra and Michael!" Damian said with a smile and took my hand once more.

"So you all ready to go back to the house?" Damian asked as he turned to look at his family.

"Damian…we all need to get our other luggage though!" Joan reminded him.

"Of course just so excited you all are here!" he said as he turned to look at me and kissed my cheek.

Damian and I led his family over to baggage claim as my nieces and nephew followed closely behind us all. Shortly after we were all headed to my car. A couple of Damian's family members rented a couple mini vans and soon everyone was following Damian and I back to our houses.

Damian pulled up in my driveway and everyone started bailing out of the cars. All the kids immediately jumped on Damian no sooner we got all the bags in the houses. Damian's Mum and Dad were going to stay at my house while the brother and sister's families would be staying at Damian's. Damian and I made plans that everyone would eat at my place given that my kitchen was a lot bigger than his.

I was in the kitchen getting ready to fix some dinner when Damian came up behind me and wrapped his arms around my waist and placed a gentle kiss upon my neck. Damian took in the scent of my perfume when he turned me to face him. I turned to face Damian when he ran his hand past my cheek and then held my chin up and planted the most passionate kiss upon my lips and then he pulled back to look in my eyes and to embrace me.

"So how do you like my family so far…and Kayla I really do want to thank you for all you are doing for me…I truly appreciate it too my love!" he said as he hugged me and gave my buttocks a gentle squeeze.

"Your welcome my love…thanks…I think your family is great!" I said softly to him as we softly touched our noses.

"So does this mean my baby boy…is officially off the market?" Joan asked as she walked into the kitchen to see if she could help out.

"Of course…who knows perhaps there might be wedding bells soon!" Damian said with a childlike smile as he brought a tray of goodies out of the kitchen and placed them on the bar.

"Kayla dear can I help you with anything?" she asked as she dipped a carrot stick in the ranch dressing.

"You know I can't remember the last time I saw Damian so happy!" Joan went on.

"Sure if you would like to help…I won't turn down the help…besides it gives me a chance to know you better!" Kayla said as she stood with her back facing the countertop.

~*~

CHAPTER FORTY-SEVEN

"Kayla...I'm really happy you are with Damian even though...he is going through that whole Beth thingy!" Joan went on as we started to prepare dinner.

"I love your son so much...I mean I couldn't see my life without him being in it!" I continued pouring my heart out to her.

"You mean...you don't have a problem with him...possibly having a baby with someone else!" Joan said with a shocked look on her face.

"Why should I...I mean I have kids too that I'm taking care of...if the child is his I will love it like it was my own...because it is a part of Damian!" I continued talking to Joan.

"You wouldn't keep him from seeing the baby!" she said with a shocked look on her face again.

"No...why is that so hard for you to understand...for instance I have kids too...I mean they aren't mine...I didn't give birth to them...I got the kids because my oldest sister and husband were lost in a car crash...and well my sister Jackie...willed them to me...god bless her soul...but Damian accepts them as if they were my kids by birth...so who am I to keep Damian from having a relationship with his child...I would accept it and not stand in the way...because the child is a part of Damian...and I am in love with your son!" I said to Joan with a smile.

"Oh god…you are such an angel…my son is extremely lucky to have a lovely lady in his life…that loves him like you do…I would be so completely honored to have you in our family…if my son decides to marry you…I just have a good feeling that he will marry you someday…I never have seen Damian this happy before…he has been having a rough time because of that Beth girl…I swear she is nothing but trouble…I remember Damian calling me after he found out…he swears he never slept with that girl…I remember him telling me he has met the woman of his dreams…and how he had to break it off because this girl was threaten by the new woman he had met…he was fearing for her life because of that Beth girl…and somehow that Beth girl drilled it in his mind that the new woman…would never accept him having a child with another woman…so what did my son do…he was fearing for the woman of his dream life…he decided he would break it off with the new woman in his life…it broke his heart so badly…you know I'm glad he decided not to let that Beth rule his life anymore…he loves you Kayla…he always has since the day he met you…Damian was pretty messed up…he couldn't sleep or eat…or function without you…that is why I truly believe he is going to marry you…he is just waiting until he sorts things out with Beth…Just do me a favor watch yourself…Beth is so dangerous…not only do I worry about my son…I worry about you too Kayla!" Joan went on as Damian's prior actions became excusable in my eyes.

"I promise to take care of all of us…don't worry Joan!" I said as I was trying to convince her.

"You better…I want to come back here again…because my son marries the woman he truly loves!" Joan said with a smile as we continued cooking dinner for our hungry gang.

Shortly after Joan and I were ready to serve dinner to all of our clan.

We all sat around the dinner table and ate as Damian started rubbing his stomach as to say he truly enjoyed the dinner he had just eaten.

Soon after dinner Trish and Tracy started cleaning up from dinner while the rest of us retired into the living room and waited to start a movie after double t's were done cleaning up from dinner. Damian and I snuggled up with each other on the living room floor with all the kids and began watching a movie as Joan sat on the couch next to her husband Robert.

We were halfway into the movie when I started feeling sick at my stomach and I took off running for the bathroom down the hallway.

"Honey…are you okay…what's wrong baby?" Damian asked through the door. I didn't answer so it worried Damian that much more he was coming through the door weather I liked it or not. I finally had enough strength to unlock the door to let Damian inside the bathroom with me.

Damian saw me tossing my cookies and he knelt down to see what he could do to help me as the look on his face became more worrisome.

Damian saw a washcloth and wet it with cool water and placed it on the back of my neck as he tried moving my hair out of the way.

"Kayla…baby are you okay…what's wrong with you?" he said with worry on his face.

"I don't know honey…I have felt this way for a while now…hopefully the doctor will let me know on Monday!" I said trying to ease his tension.

"I have a feeling the Doctor is going to tell you…that you are going to have a baby…I bet you are pregnant!" Joan said with such happiness wrote across her face.

"No way…Mum…Kayla and I have been using protection!" Damian started to say until he realized that in fact that they haven't been using anything.

~*~

CHAPTER FORTY-EIGHT

Joan saw the look on Damian's face and realized that Damian wasn't being truthful.

"You two haven't been using anything have you?" Joan looked over at her son with a slight grin on her face. That has always been something she has drilled in all her kids head use protection but like other kids they never listened to her. Damian helped me up from the ground and we headed upstairs to our room.

"Kayla sit here…and I will run your bath water okay love!" he said as he laid me back against the bed. Before getting up he looked deeply into my eyes and I watched a smile come across his lips.

"Do you really think…my mum could be right…and you might be…you know!" he started to say but couldn't get the words to come out right.

"I really don't know love…we haven't exactly been using protection!" I informed Damian as a smile cross my lips.

"I guess you got a point there…I guess it wouldn't be so bad for us to have a baby…what do you think sweetie?" Damian said as he thought about the possibility.

Damian kissed my lips and went off in the direction of our bathroom as I laid there thinking about everything. Could Damian and I possibly be pregnant and I started thinking that maybe I wouldn't be a good mommy or could I really handle being a mommy but then again ever since I had my nieces and nephew I've been a mom would it be that much more different then what I'm already doing.

Later on that night Damian and I retired to my room for the night as everyone else kind of slept where they could as they were all too tired to walk over to Damian's place. Damian closed the door behind us as he stood there just looking me as I started undressing.

"What?" I asked as he looked at me.

"Nothing you are just so beautiful…I like watching you take off your clothes…is that so wrong…you are my woman right!" he said with a cheeky smile.

"Of course…I'm your woman no one else's!" I said as I walked over to him.

 I pushed Damian back against the door as my lips came crashing down upon his lips. I started passionately kissing his lips as I thrusted my tongue deeper in his mouth. Our tongues started entwining with each other as if our tongues were dancing with each other. Damian let out a slight moan the deeper our kisses became as it lingered on our lips.

"Oh…god yes!" Damian began moaning again.

I pulled back from our kiss and gave Damian a sultry look as I started kissing him along his neck and shoulders as I slowly started unbuttoning his shirt. As I slowly unbuttoned his shirt I left a trail of baby kisses along his torso. Damian slowly entwined his fingers through my long silky blonde hair leaving goose bumps up and down my back. He slowly moved his hands up my cami top and along the small of my back. I let out a small moan as his fingers started tweaking my harden nipples as he lifted my cami top off of me. After he lifted my cami top he let it fall to the floor. He once again started leaving a trail of baby kisses along my jaw line. Damian then moved his hands southward and into my silky bottoms and gave my butt a gentle squeeze.

"Ooo!" I mumbled.

"You liked that didn't you?" he asked as he moved his hands around to the front of my pants.

He slowly inserted his fingers deep within…as the other hand rubbed my spot. Once again my lips came crashing down on his soft lips. As we kissed Damian grabbed behind my knees and pulled me up into his arms and he started carrying me over to the bed, where he gently pushed me against the bed. He kissed my lips tenderly as he slowly pulled my pj's off my body. He stood back to take in the sight of me as he removed my thongs off my hips.

~*~

CHAPTER FORTY-NINE

Damian started from my feet up leaving trails of baby kisses along my inner thighs and then his lips came crashing down upon my most private spot where he then began moving in circular motions with his tongue.

"Oh...god yes...yes!" I moaned as I ran my fingers through his spiky black hair.

The pleasure that man's tongue was bringing me was almost more than what I could stand or dare to handle as I laid there tingling and quivering as I let it consumed me as waves of pure ecstasy washed over me.

"Oh god yes...yes!" my voice rang out.

"You like that baby!" he whispered softly too me.

I shook my head yes as I lay there as he held me tightly. After the earth stopped quaking I got up giving Damian a sexy sultry look he knew what was in store for him next. He let a smile creep upon his face as his anticipation slowly Started building deep inside of him.

I slowly kissed my way down his torso stopping just below his belly button. I slowly Started unbuttoning his button fly jeans he had on as he lay there smiling. I pulled his jeans off his hips as I went back up and removed his under clothing off him. I slowly grabbed a hold of his plumpness as I Started stroking him.

"Oh yeah...baby you know what I want...yes...mm!" he began moaning loudly.

"Oh...yes...yes...suck me!" he starting moaning again.

I slowly moved my tongue and lips along the outside of his growing shaft. I Started moving in an up and down motion. I could feel the jerking motion as the intensity was starting to rise trying to make its way out until it spilled out overflowing.

Damian let out a huge moan as he finally released the intensity that had built up. Damian lay back upon the bed as he starting clawing at the sheets as he grabbed a hold of me tightly. We Started kissing passionately again as we Started once again roaming each other's bodies as if it was our very first time all over again.

"I love you…Kayla!" he said softly as he Started kissing me along my neck.

"I love you too Damian…with all my heart and soul!" I said as I Started passionately kissing him.

Damian rolled me on to my back as he began pulling himself over me until his body covered mine. He then pulled the blankets up over us and then he Started entwining our finger until he held my hands in his.

We began kissing each other again while he griped my hands tighter as he placed them above my head. With a quick thrust he was deep inside of me. Damian Started thrusting his hips until he couldn't go any deeper as we both Started moaning softly.

"Oh god yes…make love to me!" I found myself practically begging like a child for a piece of candy.

Damian Started penetrating me harder and deeper then he backed off a wee bit and Started thrusting faster and faster making our deepest ecstasy awaken fighting its way to the surface as the orgasmic bliss made our bodies quiver with pure delight. After we made love we held each other tightly giving into the slumber that was beckoning to us allowing our sleep to come.

CHAPTER FIFTY

Early the next morning Damian and I woke up and Started breakfast early for everyone. Afterwards we went over to his place to meet up with the party planner. Damian gave the man instructions as to what to do and where Damian wanted the decorations. Damian was so excited to give his Mum and Dad an anniversary party for once. Damian and I stood back and watch how his pool area was transformed in to an authentic Hawaiian Luau. Damian and I and the rest of the family pitched in to insure everything would be ready for party. Damian was very slick, as he had sent his parents to his and her spa day make over at a local Day Spa.

We didn't expect his parents any time soon Damian had made sure of that part. The party was going to be later on that evening. The party planners were perfect they took care of every last detail including the hula dancers. Finally, everything was in place when we all broke up to all go get ready for the party. Half of the family got ready at Damian's house and half followed Damian and I over to my house. We all got ready and were on our way over to Damian's place. There were just a few minor details we needed to do. Jena, Meghan and Ben were at the top of the stairs decorating the banister when a short blonde skinny lady came through the front door. They noticed she was carrying a bag and she seem nervous and out of place.

"I wonder who that is?" the kids asked all at once.

"Maybe it is someone for the party!" Ben said trying to reassure his sisters.

"Maybe but maybe not...I'm going to go ask Aunt Kayla and Damian!" Jena said in a matter of fact way.

Jena was just about to make her way over to the back stairs that went to the kitchen when they all saw the lady go back outside. She seems to be outside for a little bit when she reappeared but this time she had a big stomach. The kids took a double take and now they seemed more worried about this person.

"Let's go tell Damian and Aunt Kayla...that lady is up to something!" Ben said as he led his sisters to the back staircase and made their way into the kitchen and saw Damian and Aunt Kayla wasn't anywhere to be found.

~*~

CHAPTER FIFTY-ONE

The kids were looking all over the place trying to find either Damian or their Aunt Kayla.

"Are you sure you are okay love?" he asked me as he placed the wet washcloth on the back of my neck.

"I don't know honey...I can't handle get sick another...if I do it will be too soon!" I said in between my heaving spells.

"Kayla...I'm not so sure about this whole pregnancy...I hate you being sick all the time love!" he said with such concern in his voice.

"Look honey...I may not like this but I will get used to it...it only three more months!" I said with a giggle.

"What...you are kidding me right!" he said with surprise in his voice.

"I wished I was when Jackie got pregnant each time...she was sick for the first three months!" I said in a matter of fact way.

"You don't say...man this is so not fair to you!" he whispered softly as he squeezed my hand gently.

"Thanks...I think I'm okay for a wee bit!" as I touched Damian's cheek softly.

"Okay...let's get you to your feet!" he said with a smile as he kissed my cheeks.

"Oh…god look at the time…your parents are due back any minute now!" I said shocked as to where the time went.

"It's that time shall we beautiful!" he said as he took my hand and we walked up to the front of the house.

"Thanks…but I really don't feel all that beautiful at this moment!" I said with a slight smile.

Just as we made it to the front a car pulled up outside letting Joan and Robert out.

"Mum…Dad…how was your day…did you like it?" he questioned both his parents.

"Thank you dear…oh my god your Dad and I had an awesome time …we truly appreciated it son!" Joan said as she began hugging Damian.

"Okay…umm Kayla and I thought we all could have a nice dinner here…follow me Mum and Dad!" he said as he led them inside his house.

"Surprise!" everyone screamed in unison.

Joan and Robert jumped as they Started looking around at all the people and their other relatives Damian had invited.

Damian walked his parents to the back yard as the crowd Started mingling. Just then the kids saw Damian and the walked over to Damian to let him know about the lady.

"Damian we need to talk to you!" Jena pulled him over to where the other two were.

"What's up…loves!" he asked as he turned to face them.

"Damian…we were upstairs…we saw this short blonde lady…she just really gave us a weird feeling…we thought maybe she doesn't belong here!" Jena went on.

"Where is this lady…do you know where?" Damian started questioned them.

"We saw her around the front door was the last time!" Jena said recalling where they saw her.

"Okay do me a favor…if you see her again alert me…look your Aunt Mac isn't feeling well again…so I really don't want to leave her for long periods of time okay!" he said with such worry in his eyes.

~*~

CHAPTER FIFTY-TWO

"What's the matter with Aunt Mac?" Jena asked as she became upset.

"Oh don't worry it is nothing!" he said as he hugged the kids.

Beth had got herself some food and a drink as she sat down at a table in the very back observing the crowd. Beth Started looking around when she spotted the same woman she had seen in Damian's arms a few days back. She was bent on making this woman pay for standing in the way between Damian and her. The lady was quite stunning with her long blonde hair and her flawless skin and her very fit skinny body.

She was dressed in a floral mini skirt and a white halter-top and a pair of low-heeled sandals. Beth saw Damian walked up behind her and wrap his arms about her waist. The lady snuggled up under his chin as a smile crept across his lips. Damian was still behind her holding her in his arms and began to talk to the crowd of people as he Started patting the lady's belly. This made Beth's blood boil when she saw the attention he was giving to this girl.

The girl turned around to face him as he scooped her into a loving embrace and gently squeezed her buttocks as he got a look of lust in his face. Then she saw the lady walk away from him as he took a seat at a table with a few other people sitting there. This was it Beth began following this lady as she went inside and up the stairs to Damian's room. Kayla walked into Damian's bedroom and into the bathroom.

Beth walked into the same room and walked to the other side of his bed watching what this woman was doing in the reflection in Damian's mirror. She slowly crept closer to the bathroom when the floor began cricking. Kayla heard the sound and stopped for a few minutes to see if she could hear it again.

"Hello is anyone there?" she asked the blackness.

"Damian…honey is that you…this is so not funny!" Kayla asked as she walked out into the blackness.

Kayla was getting more nervous by the minute she kept hearing noises but she was unsure where they were coming from. She crept out into Damian's room and Started looking around. When Kayla stepped out she saw some movement flutter in the darkness.

Damian was getting a little worried that Kayla hadn't made it back yet he decided to go in search of her.

"Mum…Dad…I will be right back…I'm going to go check on Kayla…I'm a little worried she had gotten sick right before you came home!" he said with worry apparent on his face.

"Who's there…this is not funny!" Kayla called out to the dark.

Without warning something lunges forward at her and Kayla was knocked against Damian's dresser breaking the mirror.

"He is mine bitch…he is not yours…you little whore!" the person screamed at her making contact with Kayla's back of her head.

In the darkness Kayla let out a scream trying to get this person off of her.

"Get the hell off of me…Damian!" she shrieked.

Damian heard the glass breaking and Kayla screaming as he dropped his glass against the Mexican tile that covered pool area.

Kayla tried to squirm away when the person put all their weight on Kayla as their hands came in contact of Kayla face also began choking the life out of her. After a brief moment Kayla began blacking out. They noticed Kayla wasn't moving anymore and took off leaving a battered Kayla on the ground.

Damian finally reached Makayla as he flipped on the lights in his bedroom when he saw Kayla lying there on his bedroom floor.

~*~

CHAPTER FIFTY-THREE

Damian heard screaming and then nothing, just as he walked in from the patio through the French doors.

"Kayla, love is that you!" he said as he stood at the top of the darken stairs.

Damian saw his bathroom light on in his bedroom and headed in his room. Just as he walked into his room Damian saw his dresser mirror broken.

"What the hell is going here?" he said out loud to the darken room.

Just then Beth wrapped her arms about his waist "hello lover" she replied and tried to kiss his lips. Damian turned around and came face to face with Beth.

"Get the fuck off me...what the hell are you doing here...I told you before I never wanted to see you ever!" he hissed just as he saw Kayla on the floor.

Pushing Beth off of him he rushed over to Kayla side, shaking her trying to wake her.

"Kayla, love wake up...oh god baby please!"

Beth seeing Damian's concern for this woman that was lying unconscious on the bedroom floor pissed her off that much more. She began grabbing Damian away from this girl as he was bent over the girl.

"GET THE HELL OFF OF ME…WHAT HAVE YOU DONE TO HER?" he yelled just as his brother flipped on the light to see who was yelling.

"Grab her now!" Damian yelled to his brother.

"She hurt Makayla!"

Pete grabbed her just as she tried to slip passed him in the doorway. As Damian grabbed for the phone Kayla's eyes Started fluttering as Damian grabbed her hand.

"911…what is your emergency?" asked the operator.

"Can you please send an ambulance and a police…my fiancé has been attacked by an intruder!" he replied anxiously

"I have the address as 120 Buckley Ave. Sausalito…they are in route as we speak…sir!"

"Thank you so much…please hurry my fiancé is pregnant!"

Hearing the commotion through the open balcony doors Damian's parents, Layne and sister came running.

"OMG…what happening in here…please keep the kids downstairs?" Layne Started fretting just as they reached the bedroom door along with Trish.

When Damian looked between Kayla and then Beth he noticed that Beth's stomach seems lopsided as a strip of Velcro was hanging down from Beth's shirt she was wearing. Just as Damian noticed Peter was grabbing at the strip of fabric.

With that Damian got up from Kayla just as Layne and his dad took his place beside Kayla.

"What the hell is this?" Damian asked just as he grabbing a pillow with straps out of Peter's hand.

"You have put me through hell for several months…all this time you have lying and worst yet faking a pregnancy" Damian cried out.

"I'm the one that you are supposed to be with…not that whore she can't love you like I can" she cried still deluded.

Damian shook his head and noticed that Kayla was awake and rush to be by her side.

"Kayla, love you need to lay still…don't try to get up…you are bleeding from your head baby" he replied with concern.

"Get her the hell away from me!" as he could hear Beth still talking and it was getting on his last nerves.

Just then Trish was showing the EMS and police up to Damian's room. They rush in and over to Kayla whom was lying on the floor.

Peter walked Beth over to the police just as they entered the room as they saw a lady lying on the ground that had been attacked. One of the police officers handcuffed Beth as the other one went into the room talk to the victim.

~*~

About The Author:

Nicole Kauffman-Eglinger born in 1972 in Steubenville, Ohio. When I was seven moved with my family to Davie, Florida where I currently reside with my husband of 24 years. Have 4 grown sons and 3 cats. A published author loves reading and writing. Won Best Poems & Poet of 2012 and 2013. Was published in 3 compilations put out by Noble House.

Available Title:

Falling: Popstar Lover Series Book One (Amazon, B&N, Kobo, Smashwords, ITunes, inktera, Scribd,)

Wanting: Popstar Lover Series Book Two (Amazon)

Heart Of Hearts: Popstar Lover Series Book Three (coming soon)

Changing Lives: Talent Agency Series Book One (B&N, Amazon, Kobo, Smashwords, ITunes, inktera, Scribd)

Faded Memories (coming soon)

Connect to Nicole Eglinger:

@PoetGirl37

@BookLoverNikky

FB:
https://www.facebook.com/Nikkybear40/

https://www.facebook.com/PopstarLoverSeriesBooks/

Goodreads:
https://www.goodreads.com/author/show/15238556.Nicole
_Eglingcr

Authornicoleeglinger.com

ABOUT THE AUTHOR:

Nicole Lynn Eglinger born in Steubenville, Ohio on April 18, 1972. A proud mom of 4 grown sons. Resides in Florida, USA with her husband and 3 cats. Spends her free time writing new stories for all of my wonderful fans. You can also find her curl up with a good book or connecting online with my fans. Or you can find me at my local Starbucks with her laptop in tow writing my next story to share. Or spending my time travelling this big beautiful world of ours of course with her trusty laptop at the ready.

AUTHOR'S AVAILIBLE TITLES:

FALLING (POPSTAR LOVER SERIES BOOK ONE)

WANTING (POPSTAR LOVER SERIES BOOK TWO)

FADED MEMORIES (CHOLE O' BRIEN
CHRONICLES BOOK ONE)

CHANGING LIVES (TALENT AGENCY SERIES BOOK
ONE)

www.ingramcontent.com/pod-product-compliance
Lightning Source LLC
Chambersburg PA
CBHW032036240626
47154CB00003B/935